The Hunted

Brittiany West

This is a work of fiction. All characters and events portrayed in this book are fictitious.

THE HUNTED

2012 © by Brittiany West

Cover design by Brittiany West

For Chris, who never lets me lose faith.

Also for Linkin Park, Coldplay, Katie Melua, Dido and Adele, my muses.

Table of Contents

Chapter One
Chapter Two
Chapter Three
Chapter Four
Chapter Five
Chapter Six
Chapter Seven
Chapter Eight
Chapter Nine
Chapter Ten
Chapter Eleven
Chapter Twelve
Chapter Thirteen
Chapter Fourteen
Chapter Fifteen
Chapter Sixteen
Chapter Seventeen
Chapter Eighteen
Chapter Nineteen
Chapter Twenty
Chapter Twenty-One
Chapter Twenty-Two
Chapter Twenty-Three
Chapter Twenty-Four
Chapter Twenty-Five
Chapter Twenty-Six
Chapter Twenty-Seven
Chapter Twenty-Eight
Chapter Twenty-Nine
Chapter Thirty
Chapter Thirty-one
Chapter Thirty-two
Chapter Thirty-three
Chapter Thirty-four

Chapter Thirty-five
Chapter Thirty-six
Chapter Thirty-seven
Chapter Thirty-eight
Epilogue

"When the people fear the government there is tyranny.
When the government fears the people there is liberty."
-Thomas Jefferson

Chapter One
Lily

I jerked awake and sat up, looking around wildly. Somehow I'd drifted off on my pungent bed of pine needles. Judging by the sharp slant of the sun and the red impressions of the needles on my arms, I'd been out a long time.

I stretched my stiff muscles and yawned. As the sleep finally crept from my consciousness, the memories flooded back; my harrowing escape from Vic, running and trying to hide from the helicopters, my leg...my leg! I looked down and bit my lip so hard it started to bleed. The blood around the wound finally congealed and crusted over, but the skin around it looked red and puffy. I didn't know much about injuries like this, but I knew it needed cleaned.

I strained my ears as hard as I could and faintly heard the trickle of water in the distance. Since I hadn't seen any streams or creeks on the way in, I stood up to move farther into the forest. I cried out as white hot pain shot through my leg. With another whimper, I dropped down onto the forest floor again. I clenched my teeth against my tears and started to drag myself towards the water. The soil soon grew wetter in my hands, and I knew I was close.

I found it at last, a little creek that cut a path through the foliage and dirt. With one last grunt of effort, I rolled over and slurped up some water with my aching hands. I didn't have a container to carry some with me, but I couldn't move anyway. With my last bit of strength, I sat up and scooped some water over my wound, then tore off a part of my pants leg off and wiped away as much dried blood as I could.

With my thirst sated, dull hunger began to gnaw at my stomach. I couldn't remember the last time I'd eaten.

I looked around for my bag. Luckily, the food I'd shoved so hastily into it still tasted pretty good.

I lay back at last, feeling slightly more comfortable with my basic needs met. A pang of sadness shot through me as I suddenly remembered mom. Where was she? I hadn't spoken to her since the day Wes confiscated my communicator. Fear gripped me as I thought again of Vic, psychotically determined to have me in his grasp. What would he do to her? Would he find her?

A feeling of helplessness overtook me as I thought of her. I needed to get back into the city, to find her, but how could I? I could barely move.

Sleep threatened to overtake me again, in spite of my worry, but I became acutely aware of a sudden change, almost as if the air around me had grown more shadowed somehow. An inexplicable darkness filled my body as if someone were slowly pouring lead into my stomach, filling me from my hair to my toenails. Random images flashed through my mind-the day I got caught, the fight with the beasts at the Mainframe, the last time I saw mom…they swirled through my mind over and over again, making me feel sick, suffocating me.

I wanted to run, to scream, to clean away this feeling of darkness. Sweat trickled down my back, making me itch even more. A low hissing sounded somewhere nearby, making my heart pound painfully. I wondered wildly if Vic somehow filled the woods with some kind of hallucinogen.

Motivated by fear, pushed by adrenaline, I struggled to my feet and zigzagged through the trees, barely able to keep my balance. The pain grew worse with each step, making me clench my jaw so hard I thought it would snap in half.

I ambled over a huge log and saw a strange, dark cave beyond it. The cavern reached back and twisted until I couldn't see where it led. It reminded me horribly of a huge monster with a gaping mouth, luring me in to swallow me whole. The feeling of darkness intensified so badly that I started screaming just to release the pressure. The hissing grew louder, filling my ears, my body, my heart. I couldn't shake it no matter how hard I tried. Some unspeakable power slowly pushed me down, crushing me with a massive fist.

I finally drew a deep breath, but the panic wouldn't leave me. I looked at the cave. It scared me, repulsed me even, but at this point I had nowhere else to go. I ran headlong through the dark hole, bumping into walls and scraping my arms on the rough rocky sides. I finally burst out into daylight and took another deep breath. The panic slowly faded, replaced by a dizzy fatigue. A momentary wave of relief washed over me, only to be replaced by a stab of terror through my heart when I heard a low, raspy breath to my right.

I turned slowly and stared into the face of death. A tall man stood before me, if you could call him a man. Pale, waxy skin stretched over his anorexic face and skull. His eyes sunk deeply into his sockets and burned a dull red. He bared wild looking teeth, some sharper than others, and he flexed his long, curved claws. With another low growl, he started towards me.

It took a moment for the signal to move from my brain to my legs. I angled past him and ran, the pain in my leg momentarily forgotten. Branches whipped me in the face as I pushed through the trees, my breath coming in painful gasps. I could hear the beast behind me, grunting and growling as I ran faster and faster.

The edge of a long nail suddenly grazed my back, peaking my terror. I pushed myself harder, feeling like someone was pumping boiling water down my throat and into my lungs. Suddenly, the pain in my leg came back full force, blinding me and making me stumble. My adrenaline faded fast, making it hard to get back up and climb through the trees that grew in increasingly thick clumps.

After a while, I realized the beasts' rasping had faded, then stopped altogether. I slowed, limping on my injury, and turned back. Nobody. Maybe I'd really outrun him.

I lurched over to a small clearing, desperately needing a rest, when he crept out again from behind a thick, towering clump of some kind of bush. My heart resumed its breakneck pace against my ribs, ready to burst. He grinned horribly, his yellow, pointy teeth gleaming in the patches of sun through the trees. I turned and ran again, not noticing a huge, rotted tree trunk in the way. I tripped over it and smashed face first into the dirt.

I lifted my head dazedly. I tasted the rustiness of blood mixed with the dirt and leaves in my mouth. My eyes blurred, but from tears or the impact of the fall I couldn't tell. Probably both.

A long, clawed hand grabbed my arm and squeezed it harshly as the creature turned me over. I looked up into the hideous face and felt my heart stop mid-beat. This was it. The beasts' putrid breath poured over me as he leaned closer, his eyes flickering strangely in the pale light.

Suddenly, he gasped and choked as a loud bang sounded from somewhere. Wretched little chunks of spit flew out of the things' mouth, hitting me in the face. He collapsed, and his abnormally large, bald head landed on my neck. I screamed like a possessed woman and wriggled away from him. His head dropped limply onto the ground. A huge, gaping wound in his back oozed dark, muddy-looking blood. The sight made me gag as memories of that horrible day in front of the Mainframe flashed through my memory again.

I looked around to find the attacker. To my left stood a strangely wild-looking woman with a gun in hand, still smoking and pointed at the creature. Her eyes darted from him to me.

"Who are you?" she asked sharply.

I couldn't speak. I just blinked stupidly at her. She ran towards me and I tried to say something, but someone had filled my mouth with plaster. My head pounded as the ground started to tilt and darkness crowded the edge of my vision. I felt her cold hand clasp mine as I fell back against the dirt into the welcome darkness.

Chapter Two
Elaine

Elaine paced Annie's lavish living room, her heart racing in panic. It had been a week since Lily's communicator mysteriously cut out, and she hadn't been able to reach her again. Annie walked down the stairs, dressed as usual in some frilly, frivolous outfit. Elaine had allowed Annie to make her a project, and gone through a new dyed hairstyle that completely eliminated the grays, new acrylic nails, a complete body wash and wax and a new wardrobe, but everything seemed so wasteful in light of her worry. None of it truly mattered now.

"Still worried about Lily?" Annie inquired. Elaine tried not to roll her eyes. They'd been great friends when they were kids, but Annie had grown used to the lap of luxury. They had almost nothing in common anymore, and the childhood friendship slowly fizzled and faded until tension between the two became unbearable at times.

"Well, she is my only child," Elaine countered, trying not to sound agitated. "I've got to find her. Who knows what's happened?"

"Oh, I'm sure it'll all blow over soon. Come have tea," Annie implored, but Elaine waved her away impatiently. Annie meant well, but she'd been so disconnected from real life that she had no idea what the Mainframe had done, or how derelict the world had become. Elaine put down her communicator after what seemed like the thousandth unsuccessful call and paced some more. She knew by the way Wes had looked at her daughter and treated her that he was deeply in love. The thought, though a little unnerving, was oddly comforting at the same time. Elaine knew Lily would be cared for, yet she couldn't ignore the dark feeling in the pit of her stomach for the past few days. Lily had grown up so fast, and Elaine felt helpless knowing she couldn't protect her on her own anymore. She'd known that when she sent Lily away, she'd be safer far away from the city, but the constant worry still haunted her. She wondered if perhaps she'd pushed her to stay, she'd at least know where Lily was now and if she were safe.

Elaine, unable to stand the awful feeling that something was wrong any longer, rushed upstairs and packed the few belongings she had in a small suitcase. She formed a plan as she threw some clean shirts and bottoms into the silk-lined case. The trains north were always coming and going. She'd just have to take one and hope luck was with her. Annie pouted when Elaine came down the stairs with her things in tow.

"You're...going?" she asked, looking completely crestfallen. For a moment, Elaine felt a surge of pity for the poor girl. Her husband hadn't been in since she'd gotten here except for a few random stops between business calls. He ran a couple extremely successful steel plants and was gone most of the time overseeing them. Between that and her daughter staying away most of the time at school and lessons, Annie was clearly starving for company. The iciness Elaine felt towards her for the last few days melted, and she felt slightly ashamed, especially after all Annie had done for her.

"I have to find Lily," Elaine sighed. "I'm so sorry, but if this all gets straightened out, I'll come and visit."

"But Elaine-"

"I'm sorry, but I really have to go," she replied. "Thank you for all you've done, Annie, you've no idea how much I appreciate it."

"Elaine, you don't even have any money," Annie said, following after her.

"Well, I can always beg, borrow or steal," she replied, using the old adage with a grin.

"Nonsense," she replied, digging into her purse. "If you're going to leave, at least let me help you."

Annie pulled a few twenties from her purse and shoved them into Elaine's hand. "Here. Just please stay safe."

With that, she gave Elaine an awkward hug and pulled away, wiping tears. "Please come back when you find her and visit. It's...been really nice to have someone else here with me."

Elaine felt awful again, watching this grown woman plainly beg for someone to love her. She clasped Annie's hand and nodded reassuringly, though she felt oddly doubtful she'd ever see the rich housewife again. Something was very wrong. She knew it, and she had no idea what would happen or where she would find Lily, but she knew she had to find her.

With another quick hug, Elaine thanked Annie and left, striking out for the town on foot. Annie offered to have her chauffer drive Elaine, but she knew precious minutes would be wasted if she waited for him to pull the big, expensive car out of the garage, then get out himself so he could insist on opening the door.

Elaine left, trying to ignore her guilt, and bustled down the street, probably looking strange to everyone that passed by. The little town was full of people who'd made their money in industry, people who'd lived comfortably most of their lives. Though she'd been dressed and pampered like them, she felt even more awkward and out of place as they nodded pleasantly to her.

As Elaine neared the outskirts of town, a taxi drove down the narrow road towards her and she hailed it, wishing she'd worn her old practical loafers instead of these ballerina slippers Annie had insisted on buying. The driver made quick time to the train station, and she still had quite a bit of money left over after the fare, so she bought a quick meal to eat before the morning train pulled in.

She stepped up to the ticket counter and asked for a ticket on the northern train. The man gave her a funny look, asked her name again, then slowly handed her a ticket. The incident struck Elaine as odd, but in her hurry, she didn't have time to worry about it.

She sat down on the bench and rested her weary feet, all the while keeping a sharp lookout for the northern train to pull in.

A train from the capitol pulled in across the station, but she didn't pay it much attention. Trains were always coming in and out of the capitol. Suddenly, however, a group of uniformed men poured out of the doors, guns aloft. Everyone in the bustling station suddenly stopped what they were doing and stared, a tense silence in the air. Elaine sat up, suddenly alert, and looked at them, her heart pounding. Did they think Lily was here? Were they stopping in every city on the line? The thought threatened to strangle her with panic, but it was nothing to what she felt when they suddenly started stopping everyone and searching them.

She stood up and paced, wishing desperately for the train to come, but the minutes ticked by infinitely slowly. The group of men drew closer and closer to where she stood. She looked around desperately, wondering where she could go, but she knew running would only draw suspicion. Above all else, she had to protect Lily.

The men stopped abruptly as the one who seemed to be the leader pressed his finger against his ear, evidently trying to hear some kind of inner-ear radio.

"She's here?" he said. "You're sure?"

He listened for an answer, then mumbled some instructions to his men. They fanned out and doubled their efforts, checking something about each person. One got close enough for her to see that they were checking ID on communicators. Elaine tried to hide her panic as she suddenly remembered the personal tracking devices in the communicators. She dug down into the new patent leather bag Annie had bought to find it. Her hands finally closed around the cold plastic, but before she could throw it and destroy it, a gruff voice nearby demanded to see it.

Elaine looked slowly up at the man, his features hidden by a heavy helmet and tinted glasses. He frowned down at her until she felt she would scream in terror.

"Your communicator, miss," he barked again, his white gloved hand held out, waiting for the device. Slowly, she handed it over, a look of dread crossing her face. He looked at it casually, then did a double take as he read the name on the ID.

"Elaine Mitchell?" He frowned down at the ID, then pushed a few buttons to pull up her photo. He compared the two and nodded affirmatively. He then shouted to the others, who rushed over to confirm his find. Elaine sank against the cold metal bench in total defeat.

"Elaine Mitchell, you are under arrest for aiding and abetting a known criminal. You will be taken to the Mainframe to be tried for your crimes against the government."

Chapter Three
Wes

The morning dawned cold, for a summer day. Wes woke and rubbed his eyes wearily, trying to piece together the events from the day before. Random images, the beach, the small cave, the rover all rolled through his mind, mingled intermittently with images of Lily.

Lily. He opened his eyes and sat up at the thought of her, a new terror gripping him as he wondered what happened to her. If she'd stayed in the cave, she might have made it back to grandma's after they'd taken him. If not…he shuddered at the thought of it. Knowing her, she might have gone after the guys in the rover, but he couldn't be sure.

"All right, scum, up you get," said a gruff voice from in front of the bars of Wes's cell. He looked up blearily at a large man in uniform with a huge, bristly mustache. The stranger stared down at Wes coldly, a triumphant look on his face. "Vic and the others are waiting."

Vic. The name sent tremors of anger through his body. As he stood and stretched his aching muscles, he determined to beat Vic senseless for everything he'd done to Lily.

With a rough shove, the guard pushed Wes into the dim hallway and down the corridor to the lobby door. A group of about thirty or so sullen faced guys stood there, some pale white and trembling, others defiantly arrogant. Wes fell in line with them as the front door to the prison opened. Another tall, obscenely muscular man with sharp, cruel eyes stepped before the recruits and glared.

"You boys have a special assignment, seeing as how you thought yourselves above the draft," he barked. Some guys in the line jumped at his sudden pronouncement. Wes remained still, but still swallowed nervously, wondering what horrors could possibly await them.

"Come with me."

The man led the boys out of the prison, through the barbed wire gates to a waiting bus. They climbed in, single file, as the man watched each of them carefully. Wes paused, thinking of Lily again, until the muscular guard pushed him onto the bus. The bus roared to life, taking them through more barbed wire gates. Wes stared through the window dully, wishing so badly he hadn't failed Lily miserably.

The new soldiers arrived at the Mainframe, the hated building Wes had dreaded walking into for the past six weeks. Only now, instead of an employee, he'd become a prisoner.

The man led everybody to a room in the Mainframe where they were shaved clean, their hair buzzed short, and ordered to dress in uniforms. When they finished, the soldiers stood waiting for the next instruction. Wes clenched his teeth and fists, wanting to punch someone but restraining himself in better judgment.

At last, a man stepped from the shadows, dressed in an expensive suit that clashed against his unwashed hair and unkempt, unshaven appearance. His shiny designer shoes clicked loudly on the floor as he went from one end of the line to the other and back again. Finally, he stopped before Wes.

"You." He looked at Wes with his hideous black eyes, completely devoid of soul.

"Me," Wes muttered defiantly before he could stop himself. He felt a flicker of fear as Vic stepped even more uncomfortably close.

"You're the one who was with the *girl*," he sneered. "You're comin' with me."

He turned and walked, but Wes refused to follow. Fear rose in him at the realization that Vic knew far too much about them. He couldn't say or do anything that would incriminate her more, yet he felt trapped.

"If you're not going to follow orders, perhaps Chinner can convince you some more," Vic hissed. Without warning, a white hot pain suddenly slashed across Wes's back, making him fall to his knees in pain. He bit his tongue and managed not to cry out, but the pain coursed and throbbed through his limbs, making him double over. Suddenly, Chinner yanked him to his feet. Vic stared into Wes's taut face, his teeth bared, his eyes bulging manically.

"You ready to follow orders, boy?"

Wes shoved him off and left the line, angry, but not wanting another taste of the whip. Vic smirked in satisfaction as he smoothed his grease-ridden hair. Two guards stepped in line beside

Wes, ensuring he wouldn't try to pull anything again as he followed Vic, both showing off their heavy rifles menacingly.

They followed a few corridors to an elevator. Instead of stopping on the floor with the Defense Department, however, they rode to the top floor.

"But..." Wes started. Vic smiled evilly.

"Yes, we're going to the penthouse, where the president resides," he said, a look of smug triumph on his face. "Didn't you hear? President Rhone died rather suddenly, and the vote of the Mainframe was unanimous. You may call me *President Channing*."

Wes shook his head slightly, sure that his hearing wasn't quite right. But as they left the lift and started across to the hall to double doors emblazoned with the words "President Victor Channing," his heart dropped to the floor. *How could this have happened?* he wondered.

Vic walked around the huge, polished, walnut desk and sat down contentedly, pouring himself a generous measure of whiskey, as usual.

"I thought you might want to know we captured your girlfriend," he said with a cold laugh. Wes's knees threatened to give way, but he straightened his legs and managed to stay standing. He wanted to bolt, to find where Vic had imprisoned her, but the guards on each side made him hesitate.

"Yes, we found her shortly after we found you," said Vic. "You were the perfect bait. She even came along willingly when we threatened to kill you."

Wes took a step towards the massive desk, ready to strangle every last smug breath from Vic's body, but the burly guards suddenly gripped him with hands of iron.

"But since you tried to hide her, we've got a special assignment in mind for you," he said, taking one last sip of his drink and standing up. Vic walked closer and stood in front of Wes, his breath reeking of the alcohol.

"Espionage," he sneered. "And to make sure you do our bidding, you'll be *injected* with a tracker. One you can't just pull off like your little girlfriend did."

"What if I just decide not to do what you're telling me?" he challenged. He knew he was in way over his head, but at this point, he had nothing to lose.

Vic laughed loudly and picked up his drink again. "I was hoping you'd ask that. You see, the tracker has poison in it. You have two weeks before it takes effect and kills you. Bring the girl back by that time, and you'll live. You don't, and you die."

Wes opened and closed his mouth, looking like some ridiculous fish gasping for air.

"You're speechless, I see. It is quite a clever invention. The ah, former president thought it cruel to use these on soldiers, you see? He was always a bit of a softie, which is why I had to tolerate those stupid paralysis ones for so long. But now, we will finally win this war and restore glory to Illyria now I'm in charge."

"You're insane," Wes spat, struggling now against the grip of his captors.

"Enough," he replied dismissively with a lazy wave of his hand. Before Wes could say anything else, he felt a sharp prick on his arm. A sudden drowsiness overtook him as he collapsed to the floor.

Chapter Four
Lily

I opened my eyes groggily, my head pounding and about to explode. As my vision cleared, I noticed a rough cave ceiling above me.

Odd.

I also noticed that someone had covered me with a thick quilt.

What happened? I closed my eyes and ran through my last few memories. The forest, with its dark and twisted trees, my intense hunger and thirst, the strange hissing all around, the beast...

I sat up quickly, remembering the strange woman, but my stomach hadn't quite caught up with my train of thought. Without warning, I leaned over the side of my bed and retched whatever little food I had in my stomach. Groaning, I wiped my mouth with the back of my hand and sat back on my pillow. When I opened my eyes again, I looked up into the face of the same blondish, wild-eyed woman that saved me from the thing in the woods.

"I see you're up," she said, eyeing me carefully. I nodded, suddenly afraid. Her dark eyes held a strange, desperate kind of intensity that made me uneasy.

"I'm sorry," I said weakly. "I'll clean up here in a minute."

"Clean up? I guess you're delirious *and* in shock." A small, sarcastic smirk crossed her face. "Don't be ridiculous, I'll get it."

She leaned over and gently sponged a gash on my forehead over my eye. I sat absolutely still, completely weirded out and even more afraid, when she suddenly jumped back as if I'd hit her.

"What?" The strangeness of the situation struck me again, and I fought the urge to laugh. I didn't even know this woman and she was cleaning me up, acting like some kind of doctor, then acting jumpy.

"You...you're one of them," she stuttered.

"What?" I looked frantically at my hands, expecting to see scales or patches of hair or something like that. "One of what? What are you talking about? And who are you?"

She didn't seem to notice my sudden outpouring of questions as she hurried back to a large pot over a fire pit in the middle of the room. I looked around in amazement as I realized she'd converted a very large, earthen cavern into a kind of apartment. A large bucket sat in the corner, presumably for washing dishes or clothes, along with a wooden table and a couple chairs with dishes stacked on top. The rocky ceiling cracked in a couple places, letting in the pale daylight from outside.

I looked back at the strange woman, now clutching the side of the huge pot and staring at me. I noticed her eyes flick casually to a gun lying on the table, the same one she'd used to kill the thing in the woods. Terror seized me once more as I thought of dying in this cave, not being able to help mom or even find her. Without really thinking, I threw my covers back and jumped out of the bed. Having completely forgotten my invalidity, I crumpled to the floor, gasping in pain.

"Look, lady, whatever you're thinking, you can't *kill* me," I choked. "I have people looking for me and they'll kill you." It was a total bluff, and she caught it, but I tried to stand my ground and look tough. She slowly let go of the edge of the pot and folded her arms.

"You're one of them." It wasn't a question or anything. She just said it.

"One of what?"

"The beasts! Why else would you be here?"

I opened my mouth, ready to protest, when I realized she was right. Kind of. I closed my mouth and opened it again, trying to figure out what to say, but for some reason I couldn't bear to tell this complete stranger about my freaky hybrid-ness. That, plus the fact that I'd probably be worse to her if she knew the truth, and she'd want to kill me all the more.

"I know what this looks like," I said slowly. "But I can promise you I'm not really one of them."

Inside, I cringed a little. Technically, I was only half beast. But she had a gun! A gun she knew how to use, apparently. She narrowed her eyes skeptically as I held my breath. Of course it would end this way. After all that happened this summer, I was destined to die in a cave at the hands of some crazy woman.

"Why on earth are you here then?" She stared hard at me, looking like she wanted to bore a hole in my forehead.

"I…I'm a fugitive," I said, going with the truth on this one. "I have a sort of…talent. The Mainframe needs my talent for…arms development, but I couldn't do what they were asking me to. I swear. So, this is the only place I could escape."

She narrowed her eyes again. "Really. And you're what, sixteen?"

I shot her a withering look. "Eighteen."

"What's this special gift, then? You're only a kid. Even the Mainframe wouldn't be that cruel."

I took a deep breath, trying to buy time to figure out an answer. "I…it's a really long story, and I don't want to get into it." She moved towards the table with the gun again, and I held up my hands in mock surrender. "Look, I have my reasons! I have no reason to do anything to you. I'm just trying to get away from the Mainframe and find…"

I stopped talking, my throat squeezing painfully as I remembered mom. My eyes caught sight of my bag, tucked neatly into a corner, and I thought of Wes. I tried to push down memories of him, the man who'd saved me from the Mainframe only to end up in their snares. If it hadn't been for me, he wouldn't be in the South Country, fighting in a horrible war. He'd have escaped.

"Look, I'm losing patience," she snapped.

"I'm sorry! I don't know what I'm doing here or how I can get out. I didn't mean to get attacked by that thing!" I shouted back. "If you don't want me here, fine! Just show me where I can find food and I'll leave, I swear."

For a moment, a slight shadow of pity crossed her face. A deep sadness welled in her eyes, making her look suddenly years older.

"Look," she muttered, her shoulders sagging under some invisible weight, "I'm sorry. I just don't trust anyone anymore. I can't…"

She trailed off, her hands hanging helplessly at her sides. "You're probably just some kid scared of the draft." She stepped slowly back to whatever was in the pot, scooped up a ladle-full and poured it in a chipped mug. After helping me back into the bed, she pushed the mug into my hands.

"Here." The overpowering smell made me gag slightly.

She bustled off, grabbed a mortar and pestle, ground something and put it in the mug, making the mixture smell even fouler.

"This is an infusion of willow bark, ginger, lavender and heather. Drink up."

I looked at her uncertainly. She rolled her eyes. "It's not poisoned. Haven't I already decided I'm not going to kill you?"

I took a tentative sip and really did gag. "What did you say you poured into it besides the ginger and bark?"

"I'll explain that later. You'll want to sleep after you finish it."

I pinched my nose and took a couple more quick gulps to finish the stuff quickly. It scalded going down, but she was right. My eyelids immediately started to droop. I leaned back against the pillow. She took my cup and pulled the quilt up to my chin before everything went dark. The last thing I saw was his face, gazing at me with those boyish, hazel eyes.

Suddenly, he was there in front of me, smiling down at me with that grin of his.

"Lily," he said softly. "I have something to tell you."

I looked up at him, waiting. He smiled and walked away, holding onto my hand as long as he could. The farther he got, I saw that he wore a military uniform with "Landon" stamped below his left shoulder.

"Tell me what?" I asked, trying to reach out and grab his hand. He slipped further and further away until I couldn't touch him anymore. I wanted to follow him, but my feet felt cemented to the ground. I finally lifted one foot, only to fall down, down, down...

"Calm down," said a voice beside me. I sat up, gasping and covered head to toe in sweat. The wild-eyed woman still sat there. It felt like I'd only seen Wes's face for a moment, but it felt so real. All the hurt and longing over him suddenly rushed back, making me sick again. I leaned back against the pillows, trying to calm my roiling stomach. Though I felt like I'd only gotten about five minutes of sleep, the cave seemed slightly darker. I'd been out for a while.

"How are you feeling?" she asked.

"I don't know." A cold, awful clamminess crept over me.

"Nightmare?"

"No...not really."

"Well, of course it couldn't be. The lavender would have taken care of that."

I sat up as she lit a candle. Despite her wild appearance, I noticed that she was very beautiful. Long, brownish-blonde hair framed her skinny face, but her eyes were her most striking feature. They were a sparkling gray, like the ocean on stormy nights back home.

"I guess I should introduce myself," she said. "I'm Avery."

I shook the hand she extended. "I'm Lily."

"Well, Lily, I have to ask...are you crazy? I know the draft is awful, but running to the Shadowlands? Really?"

"No..." I replied slowly, feeling slightly attacked. It must have shown on my face because she smiled apologetically.

"I'm just amazed that you knew how to find the Shadowlands, and even more amazed that you got through the entrance. The toxins they use...well, it's just not pretty. I've been here a year and have never seen another normal human being."

"You have? But what are you...what toxins...what are you talking about?" My brain felt like a diesel engine, revving up too slowly to keep up with everything.

"Let's start with one thing at a time. You want to know what I'm doing here, right?" She paused and sighed heavily. "That's an incredibly long story, but to be short, I'm looking for my husband. The idiots at the Mainframe injected him a year ago."

"He...he was?"

She nodded grimly. "He just left one day to go to work, normal as always, but he didn't come home. After a couple months of the police not doing anything, I looked into it and found out what happened. I had to find him because..."

She trailed off, tight lipped, unwilling to say more. I noticed she'd cleaned up my throw-up spot. My cheeks burned at the thought.

"Because why?"

She looked at me, her expression somewhere between confused and depressed, and shook her head.

"What? It can't be that terrible," I pressed.

She looked at me fiercely, her eyes burning with that strange desperation again. "It *is* that bad, Lily, because Akrium slowly drives a person to insanity before it kills them."

Chapter Five
Elaine

Elaine woke suddenly as the rover she'd been unceremoniously dumped into came to a halt. As she looked out the thick plate glass window, her heart stopped. The huge machine had stopped in front of the Mainframe.

A guard cuffed her and pushed her towards the building, hurrying her through the lobby and into a lift. The elevator took them several stories up until it hit the very top. Elaine looked around confusedly, knowing that only the president's office was on the top floor. As the lift doors opened, the guard pushed Elaine through the opening into the hallway, towards another set of doors bearing Victor Channing's name, along with the title of president. She gasped inwardly, trying not to reveal the panic she felt. In her worry over Lily, she'd never had time to follow the news, but now she remembered Annie vaguely mentioning something about President Rhone's sudden death.

The guard and Elaine walked through the doors and waited for what felt like forever. Vic finally came in, his fancy, expensive suit tattered, his shoes scuffed and worn, and his normally smooth, greasy hair rumpled and stringy. He looked as if he hadn't slept well in a while.

"Elaine Mitchell."

He sat across the desk and stared at her, his bloodshot eyes filled with hatred and even a little fear.

"President," she replied icily, laying on thick sarcasm. "What's the meaning of this?"

"You know why you're here, so just tell me the facts," he muttered. "Where was your daughter going?"

"If you had a heart at all, you'd know that a mother would die to protect her child. I'm not telling you anything."

He rolled his eyes and took a huge gulp of whiskey straight from the bottle. "So touching. Well, your death can be arranged, that's no problem. But if you don't talk, her death will be arranged as well."

"That's a lie," Elaine scoffed, sounding much bolder than she felt. "If I told you where she was, you'd have us both killed anyway to make an example of us."

"What does it matter to you, anyway?" he sneered, knowing he'd been caught. "Fine, if you tell us where she is, we'll let her live for as long as we need her in tests. Then you can both see each other one last time before you die."

Elaine allowed herself a small, triumphant smile. He was desperate to the point of bargaining, and he made little to no sense. But a large part of her still felt regret and fear. Lily had risked her life, and continued to risk her life to ensure that she'd lived. The guilt bearing down on her over this was nearly unbearable. Part of her felt shame, letting Lily get into this mess in the first place, honestly having no idea where Lily had fled. She only knew that Lily had reached north, but where she'd gone beyond that was a mystery. Elaine assumed that her daughter had met up with Wes, but from there it was a blank. She considered the possibility of giving Vic a false lead, maybe drag out the questioning, but how long would it last? Eventually, she settled for staying silent, hoping he'd come back to it later so she could buy Lily some time.

"We have a spy looking for her in Epirus. Do you have reason to believe she'd go there? Any family across the border?" Vic stood up and leaned his hands on the desk, his dark, soulless eyes glaring at Elaine.

Elaine looked at him, shocked. Lily, in Epirus? How would she even get there? If anything, Elaine assumed she would have gone farther north.

"Ah, that's news to you, is it? Thought she was still in the north?" he sneered. "We got her up there, and her boyfriend too, but she…"

He trailed off, anger creeping into his eyes. Elaine, though she'd been alarmed for a second, felt a secret surge of pride towards her daughter.

"She escaped?" Elaine offered innocently.

"Temporarily," he hissed, anger getting the better of him. "It was a fluke in security, and when we capture her, rest assured it won't happen again."

He got up and paced the room, deep in thought. Then he stopped suddenly, smiled and looked down at Elaine.

"Tell you what," he said. "We'll keep you alive. For now. We'll broadcast everywhere that we've caught the mother of the famous escape artist. If she's still in the country, she'll hear about it and come running. Even if she's not in the country, she'll be forced out soon, then hear it and then come running."

He smiled victoriously and looked at his guard. "Send her to Biltmore. Lily will do *anything* to get her out of that place."

Chapter Six
Wes

Wes woke much later in a dark room, lying on a cold table. His left arm throbbed with pain. He looked down and noticed in dismay that the sleeve had been pulled up. A small but distinct lump bulged on the inner forearm. The tracker.

He lay back, feeling sick but trying not to give in to despair. He knew Lily had escaped, but he couldn't help but wonder where she was now, if she was safe. He closed his eyes and longed for the warm summer days they'd spent at the beach when nothing hung over their heads, no worries. He wished so badly he could go back in time and hold her in his arms again, but it was impossible now. He knew he'd pretty much been sentenced to death, whether he obeyed orders or not.

Suddenly, a door slammed nearby, making him jump slightly. Wes craned his neck around, but it was difficult to maneuver around the straps on his arms and legs. Someone shouted loudly, and he stopped struggling for a moment to listen, but their voices were indistinguishable. In agony, he lay back against the cold metal and closed his eyes again, but he hadn't dozed off for more than a couple minutes when the shouting sounded again.

The door banged loudly open and Wes tried automatically to sit up.

"Get him ready to ship out!" said a gruff voice behind the group of men that came in. Wes recognized the oily, menacing tones of Vic. A nervous man, looking slightly more sympathetic than he probably should have, stepped up and undid the straps that held Wes down. He led the prisoner out of the room and towards the lift, down to the ground floor, and to a room crowded with more recruits.

Wes had no time to register anything that was going on since another group of guards came into the room and led all the recruits out of the doors to another waiting bus like the one that had taken them to the Mainframe. Though it had been evening when Wes first arrived here, he could tell by the dull gray light that it was the early hours of morning.

The soldiers climbed on the bus single file and took their seats silently. Despair threatened to overcome the group as the bus rode through the desolated city. Wes craned his neck as the bus passed by Lily's old apartment complex. The huge vehicle ambled through the city center, then turned and headed for the docks. As it pulled up into a parking spot, more guards forced the men out of the bus and led them to a waiting barge. They were packed into it like sardines, lining the walls of the small room. Wes stood near a porthole and looked out, wondering what could possibly be coming next.

The same large, muscular man who'd addressed the recruits when they'd first arrived at the Mainframe came into the room and stood before them again.

"You lot will be a decoy," he said with a twisted grin. "Our man Landon here has a covert mission that he's to perform for us. The rest of you will go out in a wide formation so that the enemy focuses on you, not him. Landon, you're to get through enemy lines under cover of fire and infiltrate the capitol. From there, you'll begin your search. If you die, well…we won't miss you."

Several dark looks came Wes's way, making him feel even more like scum than he already did. He wished he could scream, that he could tell them what the slime ball was making him do, but he knew it was useless. Who was going to believe him now?

The man and a couple other guards handed out cheap, useless handguns to the others.

"Is that it? That's all they get?" said Wes, unable to restrain himself.

The muscular man strode over to Wes and glared down at him. "Got a problem with it, Landon? At least they get guns. You're not getting anything."

"How do you expect me to stay alive and find Lily then?"

"That's why you have a decoy cover," he sneered. "I suggest you use it."

Wes looked around helplessly, knowing he'd been trapped. *How can I sentence these men, people I don't even know, to death?*

Chapter Seven
Lily

A million things flashed through my mind as Avery revealed this startling bit of information; Vic, my dad, the crazy beast in the forest. How could Avery have killed that thing? I mean, it wanted to kill me, but it used to be a person with a home, a job, a family. I felt a little sick as I looked at her, but I didn't know what to say. Maybe desperation had driven her crazy. If Wes had been injected and had no idea how long he would live, I might go crazy too. But still, just being around her made me feel scared all over again.

"Oh," I replied lamely, figuring I needed to fill the awkward silence somehow. Then suddenly, I realized that Akrium ran through my blood too, and had been running through it for eighteen years. A sharp flash of fear shot through my heart. What if my clock was ticking down too? How much longer would I live? My heart began to beat crazily as hysterical imaginings ran through my mind.

"I'm sorry," Avery said, closing her eyes. "I just…that's why I want to find him. Find a cure, fix this whole mess that the Mainframe created."

I pulled my knees up to my chest, wishing more than anything that Wes was here with me. I could tell him about this, about my new fear of dying, but I couldn't tell this crazy woman who'd kill me on the spot if she knew I was in any way beast-like.

"So…" I said, trying to use my words carefully. "Have you found him?"

She shrugged half-heartedly. "No. There are two factions of beasts, or there used to be, anyway. The one here in the forest is vile. Completely bent on revenge. Some of them that aren't far gone yet dress up to go into the city and spy on the Mainframe. Their goal is to tear down the Mainframe, no matter what."

I thought of the beasts outside the Mainframe and things suddenly made sense. The man in the park, the one who'd confronted Wes and I that day on the sidewalk, even that crazy substitute teacher…they were all undercover. But most of them seemed to be looking for *me*, not dishing out revenge. I shivered as I remembered the one beast shouting about using me for a cure.

But how did they know about me? Had Vic talked that much about me in the Mainframe offices? Enough for the spies to hear? The questions swirled around in my brain, tumbling over each other, each wanting consideration. My head felt ready to explode again. I sat back gingerly against the pillow.

"What about the other faction?" I asked, desperate for some distraction from my thoughts.

"They disappeared. When the other faction realized they just wanted to live the rest of their lives in some kind of peace, they kicked them out of the Shadowlands."

I rubbed my forehead, trying to process it all. "How do you know all this about the beasts?"

"It's just stuff I've heard when I've spied on them, and some I've heard when they're going through the woods to the highway. I don't know if Trent is in the other faction, but all I can do is sneak around and spy, hoping I see him at some point."

I shrugged, not knowing what to say again, when suddenly a completely inexplicable anger rose within me. This crazy woman, so desperate to find her husband, had no reservations about shooting complete strangers or creatures who'd once been real people. Who was she to threaten and strong arm me? I could kill her if I wanted to.

"Avery, why do you just go around shooting people when one of them could be your husband? What if he was so far gone that you didn't recognize him and accidentally shot him?"

She shot me a dirty look. "Yes, the Akrium *does* make all their hair fall out and their skin turn pale and their heads swell and their eyes turn red, but I think I'd still be able to recognize my own husband. And when I find him, I most certainly won't shoot him."

"Yet you'd shoot me."

She rolled her eyes. "I didn't, did I? Can you just let that go already?"

She stood up and bustled around, taking my mug and washing it in the little bucket by the table, clearly trying to distract herself. I felt the white hot power beginning to surge through my veins and gather behind my eyes. Quickly I took a few deep, calming breaths, trying not to show Avery my symptoms. My eyes were probably the first thing that gave me away.

After everything had been straightened, she came back and sat next to me. "How do you feel?" she asked, peering warily into my eyes. My heart sped up in panic, but she didn't seem to notice anything.

"Fine," I said flatly. And oddly enough, I really did. My head still throbbed with all my questions and half-formed theories, but my stomach had settled at last. I actually felt really hungry. And thirsty. "What did you say was in that drink again?"

"Willow bark and heather, for your headache and leg pain, ginger for the stomach issues and lavender to calm you down."

Heather…why did that sound so familiar? I looked around, knowing I'd heard the name before, when my eyes settled again on my little backpack in the corner. Avery must have picked it up when she rescued me. It occurred to me suddenly how strong she must be. I'm thin, but not a featherweight. How she got me to the cave and into this bed, I'd probably never know.

As I stared at the bag, it gradually dawned on me. Wes's little dried bouquet still lay in there with a few dried stalks of heather, the same plant Deb used to clean her soil. A weird feeling, half fear and half awe crept over me. This plant could cure soil, heal wounds…wounds!

My leg!

I looked down at what used to be a huge wound on my calf, only to find that Avery covered it with clean bandage. I reached for it, but she grabbed my arm to stop me.

"I took the bullet out and cleaned it. You need to leave the bandage on for a while."

"My leg…it's not killing me like it was before. How do you know all this stuff? About herbs and all? Nobody in the city knows this."

Avery crossed the room to her makeshift kitchen, where several dried herbs and other plants lined the wall. She reached into a little alcove and pulled out a huge, very old-looking album of some kind. With a sad sort of smile, she brought it back over and settled on her stool, looking through the ancient pages fondly.

"It's a family thing," she replied. "My mother knew all about herbs, and my grandmother, and so on. This is a family plant book that someone back in the family line put together. It lists common herbs and plants and their healing properties."

"But how could you grow anything? The city's been in famine for years."

She gave a little laugh. "Yeah, the city has. Ever since the 'Split,' the people who knew how to work the land up north refused to export anymore."

"The Split?"

"You know, the Split." She looked at me expectantly, then rolled her eyes. "Oh, come on. You don't know about the Split? Didn't you learn about it in school? Or do city people not believe in formal education anymore?"

I clenched my fists against the soft quilt at her remark. "Of course I went to school! I'm not an idiot."

Avery looked a little taken aback. "You mean you really don't know what the Split is?"
I just stared at her. She ran her hand through her wild hair and fixed her gaze on me.

"A long time ago, there was a...civil war of sorts. Illyria used to be a successful producer of bombs and other mechanical warfare. Business boomed for the country until Akrium was discovered. Since the compound could build better, lighter bombs that decimated far more than the old A-bombs, the Mainframe immediately jumped on production. They decided to bury the old radioactive waste since it wasn't needed anymore-"

"But something went horribly wrong and it ruined the soil," I finished. At least I knew that much, thanks to Wes.

"Yes," she continued, giving me a strange look. "Hence, the famine. New research showed that Akrium had the power to even transform human DNA to make a person almost invincible-"

"So they tested a group of scientists who eventually became the first outcast group of beasts," I finished again.

"I thought they weren't teaching you this stuff," she muttered.

"They didn't. I heard it from...a friend." My heart lurched painfully again at the thought of Wes.

"Well, yeah, that is what happened. Only they didn't give up. They thought because Akrium had such amazing power, they'd try it on the soil to clean it up. The idiots don't know that the only way to fix the soil is to put in plants that can eventually absorb the toxins."

Even though I knew that already since I'd learned that from Deb, I kept my mouth shut. Avery seemed to be on a roll.

"They destroyed the soil even more, and put off pleas from the few farmers left to stop and allow them to work with plants to heal the soil. Since all of this happened over the course of a couple years, the Mainframe didn't want a soil solution. They felt too much time had been wasted already, and they wanted a quick cure. So the north threatened to secede."

I leaned forward, eager now that she'd finally gotten to the part I'd never heard before, but the pervading belief I'd heard all my life about the horrible northerners who lived off of grass suddenly made sense. It must've been propaganda filtered by the Mainframe in the hopes of discouraging southerners from leaving to go north.

"What happened then?" I asked.

"The north, even with its food production and knowledge of farming, didn't have the resources to become a country, so they declared the 'Split.' They cut the south off completely from any food imports and the south cut the north off from any government aid or recognition. So, people wound up in a sort of anarchy with every man for himself. The ones who didn't know how to farm got help from those who did, and eventually everyone just kind of learned to work the soil."

A fuzzy, barely salvageable memory floated to the surface of my mind, a time when my mom used to drive us along the northern coast, looking for seashells to add to our collection. I must've been around three or so, but the trips stopped not long after that. If what Avery said was true, the Split happened when I was just a small child. I supposed people could still go north, even after the Split, but the rumors that spread about the north would have kept people away. I'd really only run there in desperation, never considering all the awful things I'd heard that turned out to be completely untrue.

"So are you from the city then? It would make sense that they wouldn't tell the truth about the Split in a Capitol school."

"Yeah, I grew up south side of the city mostly. My last place was Cherry Lane."

"Grew up in the slums, huh?" She raised her eyebrows again, looking mildly impressed. "You might just be able to hold your own here."

I shrugged. For some reason, I really didn't want to talk about my childhood. Another sharp pang of sadness shot through my heart at the thought of my mom. Where was she? Did she stay with her friend, or come back to the city? Panic threatened to overtake me as I thought of what Vic might do if he found her to get at me.

"So if the north and south of Illyria are fighting, how does Epirus figure in?" I asked, trying hard to hold back my tears.

"The north's population is massive, way bigger than the southern population. Fighting them was out of the question. The Mainframe did the only thing they thought they could. They picked on the weaker neighbors who had plenty of food."

"That makes no sense," I replied, thoroughly confused.

"Since when has the Mainframe ever made sense?" Avery said darkly, wrinkling her nose. "They've had idiots in power so long that nothing makes sense anymore. We northerners tried to make them see sense, but the corruption up high had gone so far there was no hope anymore."

"So you're from the north?"

"Yep," she replied proudly. "I miss it horribly. My husband and I met there at the University in Parthin. He's a genius with genetics and got a job almost immediately after graduation with the Mainframe. I hated living in the city, but it had to be done."

"Any children?"

For a brief moment, a flash of heart-wrenching pain crossed her face. "No."

She didn't offer explanation, and I knew better than to press any further.

"So who's Wes?" Avery asked randomly, obviously trying to change the subject.

"How do you know about him?" I replied incredulously.

"You said his name in your sleep. Old flame? Or current?"

I folded my arms uncomfortably. "Current."

"Thought so."

"Are you a detective or something? What's with the fifth degree?" I shot back. I was getting tired of answering questions.

"Well, you slept for about ten hours straight. I was bound to notice *some* things about you when I checked to make sure you were still alive."

I swallowed hard, not wanting to talk about him. "He's in the south, fighting in the war," I managed to choke out.

Avery started to say something, then froze. I wanted to ask her what was wrong, but she clapped her hand over my mouth and held a finger to her lips. I hadn't noticed anything, but as I listened more closely in the dead quiet, I heard a muffled sort of tapping, shuffling noise. Then it hit me. Footprints!

Avery took her hand off my mouth and ran, catlike, around the room, snuffing out candles I hadn't noticed she'd lit. She moved the massive cauldron thing off the fire and smothered the flames with a huge blanket. At lightning speed, she moved her few belongings into crevices, covered the herbs with moss and ducked back into the little crevice where my cot lay.

"What's going on?" I whispered as quietly as possible.

"Beasts. They're on the move."

Chapter Eight
Elaine

Elaine shivered violently in the cold building as a tough man escorted her down a long hall. He stopped before a cell, laughed uproariously and shoved her inside. She stumbled to the small, dirty pallet on the floor and collapsed, unable to walk another step.

"Well, you should feel right at home," the man boomed. "I believe your crazy daughter stayed here when we had her. Maybe she'll join you when we catch her again."

Elaine's breath froze in her body at the mention of her daughter's name, and especially at the thought that they'd put her in this damp, stinking hole. When had she come here? Where was she now?

The man finally left, allowing Elaine to start searching for a blanket. Not so much as a rag lay in the disgusting cell.

"Your daughter is Lily?" said a quiet voice. Elaine looked around warily and finally noticed the woman in the next cell, huddled on her own pallet by the bars.

"Yes," Elaine replied cautiously. The woman shook and coughed, and instantly her suspicion melted away. The woman was in her sixties or seventies at least, sitting hunched over and obviously very ill. A thin blanket wrapped her shoulders, barely enough to keep away the chill. Though it was late summer, a strange damp, cold hung around the place.

"Who are you?"

"Agatha," the woman wheezed, "but people call me Aggs. Your daughter was here. That man wasn't lying."

Elaine swallowed hard, barely daring to hope. "Do you…have you any idea what became of her?"

The woman shrugged. "She was only here one night. They carted her off to the Mainframe the next morning."

The woman coughed again, beginning to shiver even more violently. Elaine reached through the bars and rubbed her arms, feeling a little awkward, but unable to stand seeing the frail stranger in so much pain. She figured getting more circulation into her could help.

"Was she well?"

Aggs nodded. "Just scared. Understandably so. I wouldn't want to be in the Mainframe's clutches. But I heard she escaped."

"She escaped," Elaine repeated, saying a silent, grateful prayer in her heart that Lily had made it to safety somehow. The woman looked up sharply.

"Yes. I don't know where she went, though." Aggs coughed and shook again, huddling down into her one moldy blanket. A faraway look came into her eyes as she sat up and stared off into space. "She went the only place she could. The only place they wouldn't follow her."

"What do you mean?" Panic rose in Elaine's heart suddenly, threatening to choke her. The woman looked distinctly afraid now.

"The Shadowlands," she replied.

Elaine laughed a little, despite herself. "She knows about the Shadowlands. She wouldn't be crazy enough to go there."

Aggs looked directly at Elaine, making her feel a little unsettled. "Where would she go? She can't go farther north. She'd have been captured in a minute. The beach wouldn't do, no place to hide. No, she went to the Shadowlands. She'd asked me about beasts while she was here."

"She did? What did she say?"

"Wanted to know if it was real. Seemed real interested in them for some reason."

Elaine's head swam dizzily. *Of course*, she realized, *she'd wonder about them, given her heritage, but would she really be crazy enough to go there?* She'd have nowhere else to go but No Man's Land. Elaine sighed and slumped over, putting her head into her hands, trying to hold back her tears. Aggs's small pair of ice cold hands reached out and covered Elaine's comfortingly, but Elaine felt beyond despair. She knew Lily's father had died long ago. A tall, gaunt man with haunted eyes had come to the door late one night, not wanting her to go uninformed of her husband's fate. He'd given the news and melted back into the shadows, disappearing once more to his hated exile. Elaine had been crushed, but had to be strong for Lily. Lily had been just ten or so then. Elaine didn't dare tell her what happened. It had been enough of a struggle to keep Lily under wraps. But now even he wouldn't be there to protect her in this situation.

Regrets rose in Elaine's heart until she thought she would burst. She wondered again if she should have kept Lily with her, tried to hide, but how could she deny Lily the one happiness she'd found in life? Wes was her rock, he'd been there for her through Elaine's sickness, the recovery, the summons, everything. As Elaine mulled over these thoughts again and again, she realized how quickly and suddenly Lily had grown up. *Maybe*, she wondered, *that's why I felt like I couldn't take any more from her when she'd played the role of dutiful daughter so long.* Though the realization was needed, Elaine felt worse than ever.

She looked up at Aggs, who still clutched her hands. "I didn't mean to frighten you, ma'am," Aggs whispered. "If it helps any, from what I saw of your daughter, I know she's a survivor. She'll make it."

Elaine nodded, hoping the old woman was right, but knowing she was probably wrong.

Chapter Nine
Wes

The boat reached the shore of Epirus a few hours later, all of the men exhausted from standing for hours on end in the small, cramped room. Though Wes had tried and tried to come up with some kind of plan to save his fellow soldiers, nothing came. Weaponless, and completely defenseless, they'd made it impossible for him to do anything but allow these men to die.

Anger boiled inside Wes as the guards gave a few last minute instructions before deployment. He clenched his fists, trying to restrain himself from punching the guys' guts out. He knew, however, that if he made a scene, the other guards would probably shoot the men or do something equally horrific.

In one last desperate attempt, he sidled alongside one of the guys who'd maintained a silent arrogance.

"Listen, save yourselves, don't worry about me," he muttered. "Don't do as they say. Fan out, but find cover."

He nudged Wes hard in the ribs, making him double over.

"Shut up," he shot back. "Why would I take advice from you?"

"I'm trying to help you," he gasped, angry and hurt by the reaction. He staggered to his feet again, hopelessness threatening to overwhelm him. The guard finally stopped talking and opened the door to the barge, lowered the gangplank and shoved the men roughly out one by one. He held Wes back, making sure he would be the last one out. Wes clenched his fists angrily and before he could stop himself, he punched the huge man full in the face as the last decoy soldier left the barge. The guard staggered back and sank against the wall, a trickle of blood running down his face. The others came for him, as he knew they would, so he did the only thing he could. With one last glance back at the advancing guards, Wes dove off the side of the gangplank and swam deep into the water, making sure none of the bullets could hit him.

When he finally rose to the surface, gasping for air, he saw to his immense relief that the soldier he'd so desperately appealed to must have taken the order to heart. The nudge had probably been cover-up so the guards wouldn't get suspicious. All of the men, rather than fanning out and purposely letting the enemy shoot them, had hidden behind various crates, taking cover and shooting as well as they could with the dinky pistols. Guards ran around the docks, trying to push them out into action, but injuring themselves in the process.

Wes, satisfied, turned and plunged farther into the water, expecting a surge of poison through his veins at any minute, but nothing happened. He knew he was being tracked, but maybe whoever had been assigned to watch him thought this was part of his plan.

He rose to the surface again and floated with the current for a ways, then struck out for shore, trying to plan his next move. He removed the heavy, military-issue jacket as he left the water, revealing a plain Weatherall shirt, his army trousers and boots. As he slogged out of the water on a secluded beach, he ran immediately for the safety of a nearby cove to make plans.

He shivered as he sat in the cavern, thinking longingly of Lily. He'd already decided once he'd found her to warn her to run, to get away from him. He refused to play the Mainframe's game, and accepted the reality that he would die before he turned her over to the Mainframe. But how to find her? He'd never been across the border. Epirians spoke the same language as Illyrians, but he had no idea how to navigate the foreign city.

At long last, he decided to strike out for civilization and try to blend in. At this point, he realized, he really had nothing to lose anyway.

Finally, Wes started out along a winding road that led through some small mountains. If civilization were anywhere, he knew it would be in the valley between the mountains.

After about an hour of walking, he finally came to a busier road and followed it. Skyscrapers, cars and several people soon came into view.

As he came to the city entrance, a group of men in blue uniforms, holding guns stood stationed around the gate. In his green pants and Weatherall shirt, he was a dead giveaway.

Not wanting to get caught, he ducked sideways and crept along the gate, hoping for an alternate entrance. When he was well out of sight, Wes left the seemingly endless wall and walked back to the road he'd followed previously, thinking hard. The gate had probably been hastily erected around the city for some meager protection. If the capitol were taken, the whole country would fall.

Wes began to wonder if Lily even was in the capitol, or if she might be somewhere else. It didn't make much sense for her to be there, but maybe she'd claimed herself a refugee and made it in somehow.

He followed the road some more, not really knowing what to do, when he came to another road. It was a dirt road, clearly not much used. Wes followed it curiously and found that it wound up farther into the mountains.

After a few miles, the road gradually descended to a more main road that led into the city in one direction, and a tall fence in the other. The fence puzzled him because it didn't seem to encompass the city. It just went in a straight line for miles on end.

As he looked curiously at the fence, he suddenly remembered that the capitol of Epirus was supposed to be fairly close to the border of Illyria. The fence must be the border.

With nothing else really to do, he turned and followed the road towards the city. If he could somehow blend in and find Lily, he could at least warn her before he…

Wes cut the thought off, refusing to give up hope that somehow he could find her and they could escape together. It was a vain hope, but it was all he had.

Before he got farther into city limits, Wes found a large puddle of mud and scooped up some of the muck. He knew now that Epirian soldiers wore blue uniforms and as such, his green pants would give him away immediately. He carefully covered them in mud, letting it dry for several minutes before starting off again. Wes knew it wasn't the greatest disguise, but it was all he could do.

The entrance from the mountains had been left uncovered and less guarded, presumably because the Epirians thought the road would be covered by border patrol. Wes walked into the outskirts among the tall building, staring around in shock. The city had clearly recently been bombed, given the state of the smoking buildings and the panic in everyone's eyes.

Suddenly, the air vibrated with an unnatural hum. A loud explosion blasted some distance away, scattering people and loose debris everywhere. Wes ran for cover as more bombs began to fall.

Chapter Ten
Lily

"Wh-" I started, but she clapped a hand over my mouth and gave me a death glare.

We listened intently, not daring even to breathe. The footfalls became louder, more distinct. I swallowed hard, feeling beads of sweat running down my neck as the beasts passed by the cave. They spoke in rough, harsh voices, but I couldn't make out any of what they said. Slowly, agonizingly, the voices and footsteps faded, until finally Avery said we could move again. She got up and re-lit the candles, but didn't bother with anything else.

"So…why all the secrecy?" I asked.

"The beasts aren't exactly…willing to share their territory. It's a prison for them, but it's also their plotting place, so to speak. And besides, you've seen what a far-gone beast can do. It might've been one of them." She lifted my blanket, letting in a cold draft, and began unwrapping my leg.

"What do you mean 'on the move?'"
She pulled out a paste made of some kind of herbs and spread it evenly over the still-gaping wound on my leg. Incredibly, though, the injury was fading quickly. My skin looked almost normal again.

"Lately, the beasts have been venturing out a lot," she replied. "I think they're finally putting whatever plans they had into effect."

My conversation with Aggs surfaced in my memory, making my stomach clench. What could the beasts possibly do to the Mainframe besides outright burning it or something? They'd probably lost a lot of compatriots and needed a cure now. I supposed it must be a desperate situation to be in. I could hardly blame them for wanting revenge, considering all I'd been through as a result of their carelessness and disregard for humanity.

As I contemplated my own fate, I realized that I'd begun to feel sorry for them. I at least had a chance, being born half human, but what chance did they have with a full-blown injection?

However, as I looked at the expression of disgust on Avery's face, I knew better than to bring up my thoughts. To her, the beasts held her husband prisoner and needed to be eliminated. I couldn't ever admit what I really was. I felt suddenly as if a huge weight pressed down on my shoulders, making me feel far more tired than before.

"What do you do here? What are your plans?" I asked.

She carefully, re-wrapped the wound in clean bandages and wiped her hands on a small towel.

"Well, for now, taking care of you." She smirked a little as she sat back. "But since I've been here, I've just tried to gather information. Now that I know there are two factions and where the other faction lives, I want to sail to the island where they are and see what I can find."

"They live on an island?" I leaned forward, interested. There were scatterings of islands off the coast of Illyria, but as far as I knew they were uninhabitable.

"That's what I've gathered from what I've heard from the others. Besides, where else could they go? It makes sense."

I shuffled back so I could sit up better. "Do you know which one?"

"No idea. But as soon as you're better, I could use the help finding it."

I almost laughed out loud, then caught myself. Avery looked completely serious. I ran my fingers across the lines on the faded quilt, thinking. I really had nothing else to do except brave the Southern province and try to find Wes, then try somehow to find mom, but how would I know where to start? I'd never been across the border in my life. I thought of mom again, my heart sick, but I knew I'd be caught if I stepped foot out of the Shadowlands. Hopefully she would have the good sense to stay put or hide if the Mainframe came knocking. I felt a little relief knowing that the Mainframe had no way of knowing where she'd gone. They'd have to do a lot of digging to find her connection up north. Besides, maybe if I helped Avery and somehow all this confusion ended, I'd be able to go back to the city without threat of death and work something out.

"You want me along?" I replied uncertainly, playing for time.

"I helped you out of a tough situation, didn't I?" she countered. "Two pairs of eyes are always better, especially on the ocean. I could really use your help."

When she put it that way, how could I refuse? I nodded, trying to ignore the sinking feeling in my stomach. Even though it would be asking for a death wish, I longed for my communicator so I could see mom's face again and know she was alright. Of course I wanted to see Wes too, but they definitely wouldn't allow communicators on the battlefield. The thought of him in uniform holding a gun made me cringe.

"Thanks," she said, smiling. I'd never seen her smile thus far, but it improved her features tremendously. Then again, she probably hadn't had much reason to smile lately.

She stood up briskly and bustled around the small cave. From somewhere, she produced a pair of faded jeans, a Weatherall top and a towel.

"Where did you get Weatherall?" Weatherall clothing was very expensive, made of a combination of fibers that could withstand nearly anything; fire, water, cold and heat, among several other things. Only fabulously wealthy adventurers or military personnel wore Weatheralls.

Avery shrugged. "Nicked it," she replied, not looking remotely abashed.

"You stole Weatheralls? From where? And how?"

"You just learn these things when you're constantly on the move." She sounded bold enough, but she wouldn't meet my eyes. I let the issue drop. After all, I'd broken the law far worse than just stealing Weatheralls.

"Anyway," she continued loudly, "you need to get up and move around or that leg'll stiffen up."

She helped me climb out of bed. I tested my leg gingerly and felt very pleased when it didn't give or hurt at all. We inched slowly out of the small alcove and into the main cave. "I'm sorry that there aren't the greatest amenities here." She pointed down a narrow crack in the wall I hadn't noticed. "You have to go down that little tunnel to go to the bathroom. It leads outside. It's not the best of circumstances. I bathe in the stream that runs by the cave, but if you feel uncomfortable being out in the open like that, we can try to make other arrangements."

"No, it's fine, thank you. I mean, as long as a beast or something doesn't walk by, I'm good."

"Well, if you want to bathe now, you'd better go. The sun is going down, and you don't want to be out in the open past sunset. Just don't get your bandage wet. I don't have any underclothes, but I usually just bathe in mine and dry off really well before I get dressed."

"Oh, that's fine. It'll work," I replied. "Thank you for the clothes."

I took the things she offered and walked carefully towards the crevice. The woods looked peaceful enough. I noticed now that the cave was formed from the side of a large cliff that sloped upwards into a steep, tree-covered hill. Several more hills rose among the trees as I scanned the landscape.

Suddenly, my skin began to prickle. Avery's warning about the sunset flashed through my mind, making me feel frozen. I'd already been attacked by a beast in daylight, so who knew how many there would be at night?

I ran to the stream and stripped down to my underwear and bra as quickly as possible. I waded carefully in to my knees, keeping my bum leg out. Instantly the part of me in the water went numb, while the part out of the water became covered with goose bumps. I gathered my dirty clothes first and gave them a quick scrub in the stream, wrinkling my nose as the dried blood and dirt washed out into the clear water. Then I washed myself awkwardly since I had to stand, gasping in shock as I dumped each cold handful over my body. To finish off, I bent over and rinsed my hair thoroughly, shivering violently as I whipped my hair back and the cold tendrils touched my back.

A loud, strange sort of scream suddenly erupted in the distance, making my heart race. I jumped out of the water, toweled off as quickly as possible and shoved my clothes on. It felt really uncomfortable with my wet underthings on, but my terror pushed me to action. The Weatherall shirt was a little tight, but I managed it as a second roar sounded. I ran for the cave entrance when the strange sound came again from directly overhead. I froze, shaking in terror, and looked behind me. I couldn't see anything. I scanned the area frantically, trying to figure out how to defend myself, but nothing appeared. I turned and ran, squeezing myself through the crevice-like entrance to the cave, breathing only when I'd wriggled completely into the crack.

"Lily? Is that you?" called Avery from within the cave.

"Yeah," I panted. "Hold on, I'll be in there in a minute."

I wrapped my towel around my head, scraping my elbows against the narrow wall. I finally made it into the main room and struggled to catch my breath.

"There was a beast or something out there!" I gasped.

"A beast?" said Avery, jumping up. "Where?"

"I didn't see one, but I heard a roar or a scream or something."

Avery's face relaxed. "Haven't you ever heard of a cougar?"

"What? You mean a mountain lion?" I vaguely remembered learning something about the animals in school.

"Yeah, same thing. They scream just like a woman."

I let out a huge breath. "Nice. I bet he had a fun time watching me make an idiot of myself."

She laughed as she stood up and stretched. "Don't feel bad. It's easy to get jumpy here. Listen, we'd better get to sleep. I want to be up early." She took my old clothes and the towel from me and spread them out on the rock floor by the fire to dry.

"All right," I said.

With that, she blew out the candle and curled up on a small pallet by the fire pit. I started to protest about her taking the pallet, but she seemed the proud type. I meandered awkwardly over to the bed in the alcove and fell asleep as soon as my head touched the pillow.

Chapter Eleven
Elaine

Elaine woke the next morning, Aggs' cold hands still clasped around hers through the bars. The room was, if possible, colder than before. She hadn't worn anything very warm to the train station since it had still been warm up north, but now she was positively freezing.

Suddenly, the same man who'd dumped her in here strode arrogantly up to the cell and threw the door open. "You're needed in the Mainframe," he barked.

She stood up shakily, trying not to betray how cold and uncomfortable she really felt. The guard led her down the hall towards the main lobby they'd come through before and out the double doors. The early morning warmth hit her like a wall, and for a moment all she wanted to do was stand there and soak it in, but the horrible man pushed her from behind. A rover stood waiting, and the guard shoved her roughly into the back and slammed the door. After a short ride to the Mainframe, Elaine was unloaded roughly and led to the hated building once more.

As before, the lift took them to the top floor, and once more they alighted and headed to the double doors of Vic's massive office. Elaine wrinkled her nose, still angry at the thought of this awful man at the head of the country. A television screen nearby replayed Vic's ascension to the position of president and subsequent Illyrian oath. He wore such a look of smug triumph on his disgusting face that she wanted to punch right through the television screen and hit him.

Elaine was led through the double doors and once more shoved roughly into a chair. Vic hurried in a few moments later and waved the guard away impatiently. As he sat across the desk from her, he smiled a greasy smile.

"Elaine," he began, but she cut him off.

"Don't call me that," she shot at him. Though she knew it was dangerous at this point to be defiant, she didn't care. Lily could be seriously hurt or…the thought was too horrible to finish. She hated Vic for forcing her to such desperate extremes.

"Now, now," he continued in his oily voice, "I'm not going to hurt you. We won't hurt Lily, either. We just need some answers. Wouldn't you agree?"

Elaine remained stubbornly silent, knowing exactly what he was up to and hating him for it.

"Mrs. Mitchell, let me be frank. This war is killing thousands of our boys. We want that war to end, but Epirus outmatches us in nearly everything. We have better weapons and aircraft, but they have more food and supplies. Their forces are better trained, better able to withstand war. If we had soldiers like Lily, think of what we could do!"

She looked away from him, sick. The man was clearly deluded, thinking that she believed him even for a second. She'd learned from the Underground that the war was nothing more than slaughter of the Epirians, when they'd done absolutely nothing. The need for power, the need to look like he was really doing something about the blatant starving in the streets must have driven him to the brink of insanity.

"Don't you have any idea where your daughter might be?" he asked sweetly. "Surely she would have found some way to contact you by now?"

Elaine kept her lips tightly pressed together, thinking about what Aggs had said and wondering if Lily really had ended up among the beasts in the Shadowlands. But she definitely wasn't going to tell this slime ball that.

"Come now, Elaine," he said. "Perhaps you're hungry?"

He held out a tray of delicate little cakes which must have cost a fortune. Incensed, Elaine stood up.

"How *dare* you?" she shrieked. "You don't have any compassion, do you? You don't want to help anyone but yourself as you sit here eating expensive food only you can afford, while your country starves around you. I'm not telling you for an instant where she is. You can torture me, kill me, whatever, but I'm not letting you hurt her."

He shrugged. "Fine. We'll do this the hard way."

He picked up a communicator and tapped the screen. "Take the prisoner away. Maybe a week with no food will help her loosen her lips."

The same guard came and took Elaine, dragging her roughly to the elevator, down to the lobby and finally out to the rover. He took her back to Biltmore and dumped her in the same cell next to Aggs. With a booming laugh, he shoved a canteen at her.

"Here's some water," he barked. "Make it last."

He walked away, still howling with laughter. She threw the canteen angrily across the cell and wept bitterly. She knew she'd done the right thing, protecting Lily, but she still felt terrified at the prospect of slowly starving to death. *Who knew what measures they'd resort to now?* she thought despairingly.

"Are you ok?" asked Aggs in her haggard voice. Her small, wrinkled face furrowed with concern when she noticed Elaine's distress. "What's wrong?"

Tearfully, Elaine poured out the whole story to her, even telling her about Lily's daring trade to save her mother's life and how she'd disappeared mysteriously. Aggs listened understandingly, nodding occasionally.

"If your daughter has heard what's going on, she'll find some way to help you. She's smart as a whip, that one."

Elaine nodded assent, gulping back fresh sobs. She felt some comfort from the fact that Aggs felt confident about what might have happened to Lily, but she couldn't bring herself to feel the same optimism.

After a while, a gruff, silent guard walked through the halls, opening doors, chaining prisoners and leading them out of another door. Since he hadn't come for Elaine, she assumed they'd gone for lunch. She sat back against the cold wall, miserable and hungry. She'd was already hungry, not really having eaten anything on the journey from the train station to the Mainframe, and now she felt even more so.

Elaine finally fell into an uneasy sleep when someone woke her by whispering to her through the bars. "Psst!"

She sat up groggily and looked around to see Aggs sitting next to the bars between their cells. She motioned Elaine over and revealed a few small pieces of something. Elaine took it and examined it carefully.

"It's a nutrition supplement. That's all they feed us here," she whispered. "Eat it quick before that awful man comes back."

She shoved the food in her mouth and gagged slightly. It tasted disgusting, but the hunger in her stomach eased slightly as she swallowed it.

"So…what exactly is this thing?"

"Dry pack food. The military uses it when they're in the wild. It tastes foul, but when it's all you've got, you take it. I managed to sneak back some rations to you."

"Thank you."

Aggs smiled wanly, her pale brown eyes twinkling warmly. "What's your name?"

"Elaine," she replied.

"Don't worry, Elaine," she said. "I'll do my best to take care of you."

For the first time since that awful moment in the train station, Elaine smiled. Though she barely knew this woman, she felt a warmth inside that bolstered her against the freezing cold cell. Aggs had given her something she hadn't felt for a long time; hope.

Chapter Twelve
Wes

Wes held his breath tensely, counting. Five minutes since the last bomb had fallen, but more were sure to follow. His ears rang, his heart pounded so loudly he thought it would explode.

Five more tense minutes passed, each second ticking by with an agonizing feeling of eternity. Finally, he uncovered his ears cautiously, listening. Nothing.

Slowly, he stood up and began to walk, his legs screaming in protest as the blood once more began to circulate in them.

He'd secluded himself in a small alcove, down an alley off of one of the main city blocks. A siren suddenly blasted nearby, making him duck out of habit. The noise wailed on for about two minutes before it finally stopped. People cautiously emerged from crumbling buildings, some crying, others merely staring at all the destruction, dumbfounded.

As Wes wandered around, his heart sank at the sight of several maimed and dead bodies lying on the streets, victims of the blasts. He subconsciously looked for Lily in each face, praying each time that it wasn't her, simultaneously rejoicing and mourning when he didn't find her. He didn't know any of these people, but he still silently grieved for them and their torn families.

The ringing in his ears finally subsided, and he could hear clearly for the first time the howls and angry curses of those who'd been injured or lost loved ones. Part of him wanted to help, but he held back, a little scared, wondering what might happen to him if someone recognized him as an Illyrian.

But as he watched people staggering about, some even missing limbs or clutching their heads, his heart gave out. He left his hiding place and rushed through the crowds, helping where he could.

As Wes helped an injured man to his feet, a stranger suddenly rushed up to him. The man was tall and distinguished looking with thick blonde hair combed in crisp lines on his head. Several badges gleamed on the shoulders and chest of his blue military uniform. He was clearly some kind of army officer, yet he also wore a stethoscope. Wes's heart sank again as he looked at the man. Though a friendly twinkle lit his clear, light blue eyes, Wes knew he'd been caught.

"You healthy?" the stranger asked breathlessly, eyeing Wes from head to toe.

"Um…yes," Wes replied, confused.

"We need you at the hospital. Everyone who's able is needed, they've got too many victims to handle."

Wes hesitated, then nodded, wondering why he wasn't in trouble. Though his heart pounded with fear, he felt buoyed by the thought of helping if he could and knew at this point, it would be best to play along and follow orders. The officer ran off to a small ambulance and Wes followed, mimicking the man's actions as he searched for anyone who might still be breathing among the rubble. Anyone they found was carefully loaded into one of the few ambulances that had been parked at the scene.

When the two had searched a wide area and found no others living, they climbed into one of the ambulances and drove away. Despite the horror of the aftermath, Wes noticed how beautiful the city really was, a once prosperous place nestled in a valley among several large mountains. The mountains offered fantastic protection, which was why the docks were getting pounded as the only port of entry, but nothing could stop the bombs.

Wes looked back and noticed the man who'd enlisted him carefully looking over victims, bandaging, stitching and administering painkillers where he could. Tentatively, Wes did the same. A small girl looked up at him, a large gash on her forehead. Gingerly, Wes wiped the blood away with his sleeve and borrowed some bandage and tape to cover the wound. He knew it wasn't much, but it would do for now. She looked up at his, her eyes filled both with gratitude and terror.

"What's your name?" he asked gently.

"Allie," she replied, her round, serious eyes still staring into his. He gave her an awkward pat on the shoulder.

"It's going to be all right, Allie," he told her, forcing himself to smile cheerfully. "You'll see."

She nodded solemnly, and Wes found himself forcing back tears. He wasn't that type, and had often made fun of other guys who wore their feelings on their sleeves, but he wasn't heartless.

The senseless destruction, the violence…all because the Illyrian government had messed up so badly and had no way out of the situation but to go to war. He looked down at the tracker on his arm and fought the urge to rip it right out of the skin. Trying not to dwell on everything, he turned to others who needed help.

"Did you look at everyone you could?" said a voice nearby. He looked up to see the officer staring at him intently.

"Yeah," he replied.

"Good. Hopefully the hospital can help. It's on the outskirts of the city, so it shouldn't have been bombed too badly."

The ambulance arrived at a large granite building and the two men unloaded the passengers carefully, trying not to jar anyone who might have broken limbs or ribs. Hospital staff met them at the doors and carted the victims in, each one looking harried and helpless.

Wes rushed in behind the nurses and doctors, asking what he could do and where he could help, despite his former fear of discovery. The hospital staff put him into a wing with people who'd sustained minor injuries and asked him to administer painkillers and help them get to sleep. But first, the sheets on the beds had to be changed, cots and inflatable beds had to be set up once all the regular beds were taken, equipment needed sterilized…the list seemed endless.

After four long hours, Wes finally sat down after making sure all the patients in the wing had been made comfortable and fallen asleep. His legs and arms burned and ached from the constant standing, lifting, moving and rushing.

Suddenly, the same soldier appeared in the doorway, looking as exhausted as Wes felt. "Thank you for all your help," he said. "I didn't get your name."

"Wes," he replied, standing up and taking the hand the man offered.

"You hungry?"

Wes nodded, realizing for the first time just how long it had been since he'd had anything to eat. The officer motioned for Wes to follow him. They reached the first floor by stairs since the lifts were under safety investigation after the last round of bombs. Several women stood in the lobby there, handing out sandwiches. Wes grabbed one and took a bite, savoring the taste of real bread, meat, fresh cheese and lettuce. He stared around, marveling at the amount of sandwiches the ladies had brought with them. Even at Gram's, bread was still scarce since she had to trade for it. Not all the soil had been repaired and she'd had no experience growing grain.

"I'm Conley, by the way," said the soldier as he started on an apple. "What's your story, anyway? You live here in the city or were you here for work?"

"Um…" Wes stalled, trying to figure out what to say. "Work." Technically, it wasn't a lie.

"Where do you work? Or I guess I should say, did. I guess everyone's in weapons production now. That's one thing Illyria's got on us. That and aircraft."

Wes shifted uncomfortably and nodded, hoping Conley would give up his chatter, but he went on and on asking what part of the country he was from and such. Wes gave short answers and nodded a lot, hoping the man wouldn't notice his growing discomfort.

Finally, as night fell, everybody either left or found spots in the lobby and settled down to sleep. Wes sat awkwardly in a chair, trying to figure out what to do. He thought about just trying to slip out quietly when everyone fell asleep, but he had absolutely nowhere to go. The poisonous tracker would activate in a matter of days from now and kill him. Yet he knew he couldn't stay here, continuously living off of these people's generosity.

Before he could think much more, however, he drifted off into an uncomfortable sleep. Suddenly, a door jerked open somewhere, sending a blast of cold air over him and waking him.

"He's unconscious, but we've got to get him talking," said a deep, tense voice.

"What's the matter?" came another milder voice.

"Enemy soldier. We need him alive and alert long enough to give us details on what he knows. We caught him down at the docks."

Wes sat up, suddenly alert and worried. He sat in plain view of the men. One, clearly a doctor, hovered around the soldier, trying to revive him. A sickening lurch hit Wes in the stomach as he realized the soldier had been with him on the barge that took them here. If the soldier woke up, he'd recognize Wes in an instant. Wes knew he had to run, but the doors were barred by the group of men.

The soldier suddenly sat up and looked around wildly at the Epirians hovering over him.

"Don't shoot!" he screamed. They grabbed his arms and explained that they needed him to talk. Wes stood up, ready to book it, and stumbled over some loose debris he hadn't noticed. All three of the men looked up at the sound. The soldier stared at me coldly, recognition dawning in his eyes.

"*You!*"

Chapter Thirteen
Lily

I woke the next day groggy, but feeling much more rested than I had for the past few days. Avery was already up, bustling around her small, homemade kitchen.

"Morning, sleepyhead," she said. "I was about to come wake you up."

I didn't reply, but concentrated on climbing out of bed and testing my leg. I felt no pain and could walk normally. Avery put down the herbs she ground and came over to inspect her handiwork.

"Well, the redness is completely gone, thank goodness, but you still have a bit of a scab," she said as she unwrapped the large bandage around my calf. "Should heal up in no time. How does it feel?"

"I can walk on it," I replied.

She checked the wound again and nodded, satisfied. "You know, from what I gather from the news boards, the draft is pretty serious, but I didn't think they'd shoot anyone over it."

She looked up at me, eyebrows raised in question, a small hint of suspicion glinting in their gray depths. I forced down the wave of panic that suddenly overtook me. She still didn't completely believe me.

"Yeah, they're...pretty strict," I offered lamely. Luckily, Avery got distracted by the cauldron thing bubbling. She sprinkled some herbs in and stirred. Then she walked to another alcove and pulled out a few easy tab cans of pears and peaches.

"It's not much, but eat up," she said, tossing me a couple cans. I recognized this kind of stuff. Canned fruit was a big staple that people lived on and one that we delivered a lot at the Ration Center. It didn't taste half as delicious as the food Deb had grown in her garden, but I ate hungrily. It was the first meal I'd had in a while, and the syrupy sugar smothering the fruit woke me more effectively than anything so far this morning.

Avery put out the fire and gave the stuff in the pot one final stir. I wanted to peek in and see what on earth she was making, but I still didn't know what to make of her. One minute she'd been ready to shoot, the next cleaning the wound in my leg, the next acting suspicious…I could barely keep up with her quadripolar mood changes.

"It's one of my many projects," she said, noticing my stare. She gestured to the cauldron. "I've been working on an herbal cure of sorts, for if I ever find Trent, but I don't really have any way to test it. It keeps me busy though, when I don't have any leads."

I didn't know what to say, so I just nodded. It was admirable, what she was trying to do, but I didn't think herbs stood a chance against something like Akrium. I thought again of the beasts at the Mainframe and shivered. Avery was just as cure-hungry as they were. Another reason to never tell her who I really was.

"Let's get going," she said, motioning to the small exit. She gathered some cans quickly and stuffed them in a bag before slinging it over her back and heading out the door. I followed more slowly, not wanting to scrape my elbows again.

She set off down a rugged, little used path through the trees with me in tow, struggling to keep up. Obviously, she'd learned over the months how to walk without making a sound, how to navigate using the elements around her. I stumbled along, barely able to keep up, having walked on concrete or beach sand all my life. I ducked under branches and had to hold in shrieks as spindly limbs clutched at my clothes and hair. I felt just like Snow White in that cartoon from so long ago.

At long last, we reached the edge of the trees and came to the same cave I walked through to get into the Shadowlands. I froze, not wanting to go further, mainly because of the memory of the beast I'd seen close to here, but also because of the caves' strange effect on me.

"Oh, I forgot." Avery hurried back to me and handed me a simple handkerchief. I looked at her questioningly. "Hold it over your mouth."

I held it up, completely nonplussed. "The cave is laced with hallucinogenic herbs. The beasts figured out how to do it, being scientists and all. They did it so that anyone from the Mainframe following them would get dizzy and disoriented and turn back."

"But what will the handkerchief do?"

"It only affects you if you breathe it in, so the handkerchief will keep you from breathing it in. Duh. Now come on, I want to get out before the tide goes back again."

I clamped the cloth firmly over my mouth and nose and hurried after Avery. Surprisingly, she was right. I didn't hear any horrible hissing or get sick as we walked through the cave. Once on the other side, Avery stowed her handkerchief and started looking around at the trees. I followed and watched curiously as she came to one with a small, barely noticeable "x" on it. From that tree, she veered sharply to the left and before long, found another tree with "ix" carved into it. Avery veered to the right this time and found another marked tree. The pattern continued for ten trees, sometimes veering sharply in one direction and sloping gently in other directions. Avery followed some kind of strange path only known to her. At the last tree, marked with an "i," she turned sharply right and walked straight ahead through two trees into a small clearing. A small cave sat on the edge of a clearing, carved into a small hill. She hurried inside to what I thought was a massive boulder. She reached down for something, and I realized she had found the corner of a huge grayish tarp. As she pulled the tarp away, she revealed a huge car beneath the tarp. It looked like an old single-cab truck, the kind people used to drive years ago.

She carefully folded the tarp and stowed it in one of the little crevices along the cave. "Hop in," she called.

"How did you…what…" I couldn't even talk. Avery was so careful, so thorough about everything-her cave, her herbs, her tree system.

"I told you, the beasts can never find my hiding spots for things," she explained.

"But the trees…how did you know to do that? What where those weird symbol things?"

"Roman numerals. I counted down from ten to one. Most people don't even know that number system anymore since its centuries old, so I knew no one would recognize it. And marking the trees is an old Native American trick. They did it so they didn't get lost in the woods."

Native Americans? Romans? I felt distinctly dumb as I climbed into the old truck. Avery knew so much that I'd never even heard in my lifetime. I thought back through school, all the things I'd learned, and realized how little my teachers talked about history, or even current events for that matter. Government classes consisted of the greatness of the Mainframe, how the leaders broke our small country away from its former controllers, organized our own leadership and how, more recently, pulled us through this famine and all the trouble with the north. Yet they hadn't done everything they puffed themselves up about. People still starved, and their anti-north attitude isolated us from the reach of more food, properly grown food instead of ancient canned goods and scraped up rations. I'd learned math and science and all, but our literature was limited to history books about the Mainframe. I frowned as I realized just how much control the Mainframe had over everything, how ignorantly I'd grown up.

Avery and I didn't talk much as she angled carefully out of the cave, through the trees and onto the main highway. Instinctively I ducked as we drove past the huge news boards. My throat closed with momentary alarm as my name and picture flashed through the ads, painting me as an escaped criminal. *Criminal*...the thought hit me like a brick to the head. I looked at Avery, terrified, but she kept her eyes on the road, thankfully. After navigating through a few side roads, she finally took the familiar frontage road leading to the beach. I felt my stomach clench, my palms begin to sweat at the thought of being out in the open again, but I tried to push it down.

We pulled up onto the beach to find clear blue skies and high, turbulent waves. Massive swells swirled and pounded angrily against the shore, matching my troubled mood perfectly.

"I wanted to try to find the island today," said Avery as she killed the engine. "The beasts are probably more friendly there. I wanted to see if Trent went there, or if anyone knows what happened to him." I nodded, wondering why I felt the need to be so mute around her. I usually didn't get intimidated by people, but she definitely intimidated me.

I stepped out of the truck and breathed in the familiar salty sea air. A sharp pang of sadness shot through my heart as I looked down the beach at the pier in the distance where Wes first kissed me.

"Lily!"

I looked over at Avery. I must have looked dazed because she frowned.

"Are you here?" she asked.

"Yeah," I replied apologetically.

"Well, come on, we've got work to do."

I followed her past the pier to a small cave on the waterfront at the point that I'd never noticed before. She crawled inside and I followed after her. The cave was little more than a tiny crevice, barely able to fit the both of us. A small speedboat sat cradled in the water behind the mouth of the cave. Avery hopped inside and grabbed a silver key from under the seat.

"Get in," she ordered. I climbed cautiously over the side. I'd grown up near the beach, but I'd only been on boats a handful of times, and certainly never one this small. The pounding swells made the boat rock violently. The last thing I wanted to do was head out onto the tossing waves in this tiny thing, but I decided not to mention it.

"Where did you get this thing?" I asked.

"Swiped it, what do you think?" she asked, looking somewhat proud and fearful at the same time.

"How? You can't exactly fit a speedboat in your pocket."

Avery just grinned instead of answering. She turned the key and the boat roared to life. We shot out of the cave and skipped over the churning water. My heart leapt into my throat as the boat got some massive air over a huge wave and came crashing down into the frothy foam.

"You sure you know how to drive this thing?" I yelled.

"Sorry about that!" she called back with a wicked grin. The waters calmed more once we reached open sea. I looked over at Avery. Even though she wore sunglasses, I could tell that her face looked less lined, less stressed and slightly younger. The sunlight did wonders for her complexion.

The sea gleamed a bright blue today, thanks to the unusually clear sky. I laid back against the seat and soaked in every inch of the sunshine I could get. I couldn't tell if it was the sun or the perfectly flowing ocean or being away from the Shadowlands, but for the first time in a long time, I felt wonderful. Maybe it was all of the above. A rare smile crossed my lips and a laugh escaped my throat. Avery looked at me and grinned.

"Feels good, doesn't it?" she called.

"Yeah, it does," I hollered back over the noise of the boat. "What is it?"

"I don't know, really, but people used to believe that the ocean had a healing effect on troubled minds. Maybe it's true."

We sped through the water for a couple hours, Avery checking her compass and hand-drawn chart a couple times. I felt a tiny flicker of fear every time she did this. I couldn't help but wonder if all her eavesdropping had really given her enough information to find the island.

Around noon, Avery killed the engine and dropped anchor so we could eat our lunch. The cold canned beans weren't very satisfying, but I knew beggars couldn't be choosers. My stomach twisted in agonized hunger. My last proper meal must have been with Deb and Wes, and before that at the hospital with mom. I'd been steadily starving and didn't realize it. I wondered again where mom was, if she was safe. I'd never wanted to speak to her or see her so badly in my entire life. Despite the sun and feeling so great, my stomach twisted at the thought of delaying my search for mom and Wes.

Avery resumed driving, her shoulders slumped with weariness. I felt more and more skeptical about our course, especially when the sun began to dip steadily towards the horizon. Avery bent down to check the compass and her charts more and more as the time passed.

Then suddenly, a dot appeared on the horizon, very small at first, but getting bigger all the time. More dots followed. I squinted at them, trying to figure out if they were shoals, but then I noticed scrubby pine trees springing up on them. They were islands. A tiny chain of islands that I'd always heard about but never been to. I felt a strange, sudden thrill of excitement.

Avery gave an audible sigh of relief, making me feel a little better. I wasn't the only one who'd wondered if we were on course, after all.

As we got closer, my breath caught in my throat. The island was ablaze with a variety of wildflowers, surrounded by white sands and turquoise waters. The setting sun seemed to augment the vivid colors, making the island seem magical in a way.

"It's beautiful!" I called.

Avery nodded, unable to reply as she tapped the shift screen to slow the boat down. We pulled up close to the shore and Avery killed the engine. She stowed the silver key under the seat, dropped the anchor and leapt over the side of the boat.

"Come on!" she said as she bobbed up out of the water.

I'd swum in the ocean hundreds of times, but I really didn't like the idea of getting my clothes completely soaked.

"Can't we pull up closer?"

"Don't be such a sissy," she muttered and swam off towards the shore. Reluctantly, I jumped overboard and followed her. The water was pleasantly warm, though, and soon I found myself wanting to swim rather than go looking for beasts, but Avery gestured impatiently from the shore. I walked up the beach, squeezed the water out of my hair, shook off my clothes a bit and followed her.

We reached a path leading from the beach and followed it up to a large, rocky field. Flowers in oranges, reds, purples, pinks and yellows grew through the cracks in the rocks, making the field look like a scattered, broken rainbow. Wind whipped all around us, drying our clothes in no time as we surveyed the island.

We started down another twisting path to a narrow beach bordered with tall cliffs. Both of us stopped and gasped as we stumbled upon a crumbling structure sitting close to the shore. It looked oddly sunken, sitting at the edge of the sand with waves brushing the stone foundation. Despite the building's odd appearance, it was tall, impressive and ancient-looking, with a large tower in the middle that had a gap missing. It looked like a giant had ambled over and decided to take a bite out of it. Huge chunks were missing from the walls and the roof was almost completely caved in. Along the side of the building sat several strange, squarish rocks in neat rows.

Avery motioned to me to follow her as we stepped inside the structure. A few random benches sat scattered among the debris. It was clear that there used to be more benches, and that they used to sit in uniform pattern facing a large, boxy thing at the front.

"What is this place?" I asked.

"It's an old church," she replied, her voice hushed with reverence.

"A church?" I whispered. "I thought those were destroyed years ago."

"They were, but I guess this one was remote enough that it didn't get touched. I don't think anybody really knows about this place."

I looked around in awe. Evenly spaced gaps ran along the walls that I guessed must have been windows at one point. I had read about churches in history books, but I never thought I'd actually stand in one of them. Something inside me stirred, a strange longing that I'd never realized existed within me. For the first time in my life, I wanted to know what exactly lay beyond the grave. I shook myself, feeling a little strange. This place seemed to have a strange effect on me. Mom and I had never really discussed religion when I was growing up, but she taught me some old prayers people used to say. Even though I prayed every so often when circumstances were dire, religion just wasn't something that anybody really talked or thought about where I'd grown up.

I sat down on one of the wooden benches and looked up at the shafts of light playing across the debris-strewn floor. A sudden, subtle feeling came over me, like warm bath water being poured on my head. Somehow I just knew my mother and Wes were still safe, but the good feeling still felt tainted with my lingering sadness.

"Lily?"

I looked up to see Avery standing close to me, looking down at me with a furrowed brow.

"Sorry, I was just…thinking," I said.

"You're crying," she replied.

"Oh," I said, absentmindedly brushing the tears from my cheeks.

"Are you ok?"

"Yeah…I'll be fine."

"We can leave if you want to," Avery said. She put her hand on my shoulder. I shook my head and stood up.

"I'm fine. I just…miss my mom." My voice cracked and I turned away in embarrassment.

"Where is she?" Avery asked tentatively.

I took a deep breath. "The last time I saw her was in a hospital up north. She'd gone there for the Barbach treatment."

"Is she…" Avery trailed off, looking at me uncomfortably.

"She's alive. It worked. But I had to leave her. I…it's a long story."

I clamped my mouth shut, afraid I'd said too much again. Avery awkwardly patted my shoulder and gave me an understanding smile. It was the first real sign of friendship she'd given. I smiled back.

"I know what it's like," Avery replied gently. "Not knowing what's happened to someone you love. I feel that way for my husband and my parents. My parents are dead, and Trent…well, you know how that ended up."

She shrugged, obviously trying not to cry. I reached out to comfort her, but I heard the creak of floorboards and froze.

"What are you doing here?" interrupted a deep, raspy voice behind us. Avery and I froze. My heart beat a rapid staccato. I turned slowly and again looked into the horrible face of death.

Chapter Fourteen
Lily

Fear froze me to the spot. Though the monster didn't look half as bad as the one I'd encountered in the woods, I felt the same surge of terror squeeze my heart until I thought it would explode.

Oddly though, instead of charging us and trying to eat our heads, the man held his hands up in a gesture of peace.

"Forgive me," he mumbled. "It's been so long since I've seen anyone...normal."

Though his eyes had become distinctly red, they held a look of such deep sorrow that I found myself feeling pity for the thing.

"Who...who are you?" Avery asked. She stood stiffly, clearly trying to hide her own fear.

"Name's Jensen. Not that it matters anymore, though."

He shuffled over to a bench and sat down. I glanced at Avery, who shrugged.

"Should we talk to him?" I whispered.

"Well..." she looked over at him, sitting on his chair and clearly deep in thought. "I guess if he were far gone, he'd have killed us by now."

She stepped gingerly over some old rubble and stood next to the beast. "Pardon me," she said, sounding way too serious for the situation, "but...are you one of the exiled beasts?"

He gave something between a grunt and a shrug. "You could say that."

Avery looked back at me, exasperated. I stepped closer and looked at the man. No doubt about it, he had the look of a man who'd given up on life.

"Can...can we talk to you?" I offered timidly.

The man gestured vaguely to the rubble and old benches scattered through the room. Avery and I sat uncomfortably on a rickety pew that had been turned about so that it faced him. He sat up for a moment and looked at us, a strange sort of curiosity spreading across his face.

"Why are you here?" he rumbled.

I looked at Avery, not daring to speak, knowing my voice would crack with terror. I'd had enough of these guys to last a lifetime. "We're looking for my husband. Trent Donovan. Do you…know him?"

His brow furrowed thoughtfully. "Donovan…yeah, I know him." The look of sadness intensified, making Jensen seem to sag. Avery nearly jumped off her seat in excitement.

"You do? Where is he? I'm…I'm his wife…"

She sat back down, her expression a cross between anxiety and desperation. I knew without asking that she was wondering if he'd died. Jensen gave a heavy sigh and rubbed his brow. Finally, he sat up and looked at Avery with pain in his eyes.

"Donovan was…is extremely intelligent," Jensen began. "He was one who lasted longer than the others. He didn't want anything to do with the Mainframe scheme the others are working on, so he got exiled here. But his DNA knowledge was too much to resist. They came here a few months back and spirited him away."

"Do you know what happened to him after that?" Avery clutched the ancient wood seat as if it would fly away. "Please, I need to know."

"I don't know. I wish I could tell you, but I've been on this island so long I don't know hardly anything anymore."

Suddenly, his back arched weirdly, making him look even more grotesque. He gave a raspy sort of yell, making his eyes flash vivid red. I stood up, ready to bolt, adrenaline already pumping through my veins, but he sagged in his seat just as suddenly as he'd had his attack. I looked at Avery, expecting the same shock I felt to show on her face, but she looked almost…pleading.

"You girls need to leave," he grunted. "I don't know how much longer I can last before I go."

"Please, Jensen, please tell me if there's anything else you know. Was Trent far gone? Was he close? I have to know!"

Avery looked on the brink of tears. Jensen clenched his long, clawed fingers and gradually let his shoulders relax.

"Like I said, he transformed slower than the rest. He and I were the only ones left when he was taken. I could tell he wouldn't go down without a fight."

Avery slumped, disappointed, but I could tell she felt slightly bolstered by the news. "Thank you," she whispered.

I looked at the empty frame that once held a door and realized with a start night had fallen. I realized a little too late that we'd gotten ourselves into a major predicament. I hadn't sailed a whole lot, but I knew it would be dangerous at night, especially since neither Avery or I were experienced sailors. But on the other hand, Jensen's little outburst terrified me. We couldn't stay much longer. I looked at Avery, but she didn't seem to catch the hint that I wanted to leave.

"Were there many others in your exiled group?" she asked. Why would she care? She got all the information about Trent she needed.

"A few dozen to begin with," Jensen replied. "Most of 'em lost it shortly after we got here. Had to shoot 'em."

He gave another heavy sigh and stood up. "Towards the end, it was me, Donovan, Briggs, Jameson, Cole and Mitchell."

I gave a start, forgetting my desperation for a moment as I heard my last name. "Did you just say Mitchell?" I asked bluntly.

He nodded. "He was smart, all right. Fought as long as he could."

"Where is he? Is he buried here?"

Both Avery and Jensen gave me a strange look, but I had to know. "Yeah. Just on the side of the church there. Near the beach."

I remembered the weird squares along the side of the church and realized with a sickening feeling that it was a makeshift graveyard. Jensen motioned us outside and through the rows of stones until he came to one near the front overlooking the shore. Someone had crudely carved "Owen Mitchell" into the rock. I crumpled to my knees, strangely overcome with emotion.

"What was he like?" I choked through my tears.

"He...he was a good man. Always making jokes, trying to keep things lighthearted even though we all knew we were gonna die. It was his idea to split with the other group, come here and try to have some kind of a peaceful life until...well..."

He trailed off uncomfortably as I wiped my streaming tears. Why did I feel so much for a man I never knew? I'd never even known what he looked like. Mom didn't bring him up much, and I didn't feel any kind of desperate need to know him, but now, looking at this sad grave buried half-deep in the sand, my heart ached for him.

"Is this…your father?" Avery asked. She sounded sympathetic, but I noticed a slight edge under her voice. I nodded, lost for words.

"It has to be. He was a scientist, one of the first to be subjected to the Akrium injections."

I finally stopped crying and wiped the last of my tears on the sleeves my Weatherall top. I couldn't stay here any longer. Jensen, the lone man left to die, along with my dad's grave, was just too much to take.

"Can we go?" I asked Avery.

She nodded mutely, a strange expression on her face. "Thank you for your help," she said solemnly, turning to face Jensen. He tipped his head towards her and gave a sad smile, but I noticed his eye twitched just slightly.

Avery took off down the beach to ready the boat. I lingered behind, not sure what to say but wanting to give my thanks to Jensen somehow.

"You don't know what this means to me," I offered, unable to look at him. "I've never known my father, just what happened to him. But…thank you for laying him to rest."

He didn't answer. My neck prickled eerily at the sudden quiet. I looked up at him nervously, only to see my fears justified. His eyes no longer held sorrow, sympathy or any emotion at all. He stared straight at me, unflinching. He flexed his claws once as his lips rose in a snarl.

"Jensen!" I cried, trying to break him out of it. "Jensen, snap out of it!"

He let out an unearthly roar and charged at me, then stopped, seeming confused. I paused, figuring he'd come out of it, but his back arched weirdly again. With another roar, he started after me. I turned and ran, my heart thumping rapidly against my ribcage. Avery stood on the shore waiting for me, but her eyes widened in panic as she noticed Jensen pursuing me.

"Run! I'll get the boat ready!" she screamed. She dove deftly into the waves and got to the boat in a flash. I pounded across the sand, my burning lungs protesting with each ragged breath I drew.

I reached the water at last and plowed awkwardly into the surf. I finally reached deep water and swam for all I was worth, but a hand suddenly grabbed my ankle in a vice-like grip. I turned, terrified, to see Jensen gripping me, his face split in a grin of triumph. I shook my leg, but the weight of my clothes and the water all around me threatened to pull me under. I tried grabbing his hand and wrenching it from me, but he was much too strong. He pulled me towards him slowly. I remembered my other leg and pushed my foot into his face with all the force I could muster. It did the trick. He howled in pain and let go, trying to stay afloat and grab his face all at once.

"Lily! Hurry up!"

I scrambled towards the boat and used the last of my strength to haul myself over into the seat. Avery fumbled for the key.

"GO!" I screamed hoarsely. Jensen's hideous head bobbed in the waves no more than ten feet from us.

"GET THE ANCHOR!" she screamed back.

I found the chain and yanked the anchor as hard as I could until it finally slid over the side of the boat. Jensen swam a mere three feet away. He reached a claw out of the water towards the side of the boat, a sickly blackish blood running down his face.

"Go!" I gasped.

Avery finally jammed the key into the ignition, tapped the gear screen and jerked the wheel sharply to the left. The boat curved through the tossing waves and shot out to open sea. Jensen's angry howls died away as we sped over the choppy water.

Chapter Fifteen
Lily

I laid back against the seat, soaking wet, freezing and trying to catch my breath. The weather had been warm and pleasant when we arrived, but now blackened clouds loomed above us, blocking out the stars and threatening to empty their contents in an angry display. The water rose in pitches, tossing us to and fro as lightly as a rag doll in the clutches of a giant. I clung to the sides as Avery did her best to navigate the churning waves.

I could see in an instant her efforts were pointless. The swells only grew larger, pounding harshly against our boat, determined to overpower us.

Suddenly, a freak gust of wind blew up, creating a huge wave that towered before us. I felt the boat splinter around us as the mammoth crashed down all around. I dove out of the boat, trying to hit the wave head on, but the force of the curl knocked me back, turning me over and over until I thought I'd be sick. I'd never experienced waves like this.

I finally broke through the surface, only to be hammered with rain. I squinted through the downpour, trying to find some trace of Avery, but she'd disappeared. My heart tightened with panic. I realized then, even despite our strained liaison, she'd somehow become a friend. I pushed through the water, using the powerful strokes I'd learned through the years against the current, but couldn't find her anywhere.

Hopelessness began to take hold. I had no idea what direction to take. My only possible compasses, the stars, were lost in a sea of angry clouds. I rose and fell with each powerful wave, knowing I would run out of energy soon.

"Avery!" I cried, my voice hoarse with the intake of so much salt water. "Where are you?"

Nothing answered but the howl of the wind and the sweep of the rain across the mountains of water. I'd always felt so comfortable in the ocean, so at home, but as I thought of sharks and drowning, the ocean felt like some former loving pet turned against me.

Mom always used to say when I was lost to stay put, but how could I here? The sea was constantly moving, constantly changing.

I had to do something. Picking a direction, I struck out and began to swim, using long, slow strokes rather than fast ones. As I grew tired, I floated on my back. I tried not to thrash, knowing that the motion attracted sharks.

After fifty or so more strokes, I laid on my back, trying to save energy, when suddenly my head bumped into something. I darted away from the object, terrified to see a shark's huge mouth yawning before me, but luckily it was something completely unexpected. Avery floated nearby, slumped over a free floating piece of wreckage from our boat. I must have bonked the edge of the piece. I swam over as quickly as I could and shook her.

"Avery?" I shook her again. No response. I moved her face towards me, shocked at how pale her face had gone. A bruise had already begun to form above her eye. "Avery!"

She groaned slightly. For a second, her gray eyes opened a crack, then closed. I grabbed her wrist and concentrated hard on her pulse. Faint, but there.

I pushed her more securely over the wreckage and pinned her arms under my own. I hooked my fingers around the edge of the wreck and started to swim for all I was worth.

It didn't take long to grow weary. My arms ached with the effort of swimming with Avery in tow. Even with my Akrium-infused freaky hybridness, my body was hitting the limit. I paused and tread water for a moment, trying to decide what to do. The waves, thankfully, had died down. The storm finally began to wear itself out, the howls of wind reduced to whispers.

The boat trip out had taken all day when we came, and the boat accident happened a mere ten minutes away from the island. Even if I knew where the island was, we couldn't risk going back there in case Jenson was still around, but it would take literally days to swim back the way we came. Not to mention we'd die of thirst and starvation first.

Then I remembered Avery's mention of several islands, not just one. If I struck out and kept swimming, maybe I'd hit land eventually. We'd have to figure it out from there.

I began swimming again, my shoulders and arms aching in protest. The clouds cleared slowly, the storm all but gone. I could swim more easily, but my body spent, I could hardly move. Any strokes I attempted were feeble at best, pushing us through the water an inch at a time. I had no way to track, but we'd definitely been in the water at least a couple hours.

I laid on my back, clutching Avery and the wreckage, and tried to figure out what to do. If we floated aimlessly forever, we might hit an island or something, but maybe not. All my ocean safety classes couldn't guarantee how long you might live in open water. They said roughly twenty-four hours at best guess.

The water had long since grown still, but small waves suddenly began to lap over my face. I sat up in the water quickly, terrified a whale or shark might be creating the wake, but my heart caught in my throat when I saw a huge boat threading its way silently through the water. I squinted at it, but didn't see any familiar insignia on the siding. Of course, it was really too dark to see anything, but it didn't matter. It was a boat!

"Help!" I cried, waving my arms around. "HELP!"

The boat continued on its path away from us. I summoned the last of my strength, grabbed Avery and pushed through the water. Twenty strokes took us closer, but the boat powered on, much faster than us. I gave it a few more strokes and shouted as hard as I could. I swore I heard a faint cry, but wondered if my ears played tricks on me. I quieted my heavy breathing and listened as hard as I could.

"Can you hear me?"

I heard it distinctly this time. The ship loomed above us, very high in the water, but the cry was unmistakable.

"Yes!" I shouted back, my voice cracking and strangled. "Please help!"

Slowly, miraculously, the boat began to turn. I cried out in relief as it sidled along us and tossed out a net. I grabbed Avery around the middle and hoisted her halfway into the ropes, but couldn't get her in all the way. Using the last bit of my strength, I hauled myself up inside and pulled her up. Her face looked worse, the purple bruise standing out against her stark white face, but I could still feel a faint pulse when I touched the hollow of her neck.

The crew hoisted us up overboard. I could tell by the uniforms we were on some kind of patrol boat, but the fabric was different from those of the Mainframe Ocean Patrol.

"Are you ok?" asked a grizzled old man as he helped us climb out. "Lucky Shingleton on aft spotted ya, or we'd have passed ya by."

"We're ok, but my friend needs medical attention," I gasped. "I think she hit her head. Our boat wrecked in the storm."

"Ar, she was a nasty one at that," the man grunted. "We had to batten down, but we made it through."

"Thank you for your help," I replied. I sat down on a nearby box, suddenly very exhausted. The sailors worked for several minutes to revive Avery. She finally came around, looking at the faces surrounding her in bewilderment.

The men shuffled us off to a cabin, got us some old kitchen crew clothes for us to wear and fed us soup and water. Color slowly filtered back into Avery's face, and she even managed a grateful smile and a thank you. After a while, a tall man with a grizzly gray beard and kind, crinkly eyes came in.

"Looks like you two had a close call. My name is Captain Davis." He extended his hand and we shook it weakly. "Where are you two from?"

"Arduba," I said before I noticed Avery's warning glance.

The man's kind eyes suddenly sharpened. "In Illyria?"

Neither of us said anything. He rubbed his chin, eyeing us warily. "You're from Illyria, aren't you?"

Epirians. I should have known. The boat was unrecognizable. The uniforms were different. That should have been my first warning, since I'd spent my life seeing the Mainframe boats and sailors in the harbor, but I'd been so desperate…

"We…we are, sir, but please just let us explain," I pleaded, ignoring Avery's glare.

"Explain?" he asked, his voice suddenly harsh. "Explain what, that you're spies? Do they think sending women will fool us somehow?"

He turned to go, his face a livid red. I had to do something. "We're with the Underground!" I shouted in desperation. He stopped and turned to stare at us.

"What underground?" he muttered.

"We're working against the government. I know what they're doing is wrong, and we're trying to stop it."

"What are a couple o' girls gonna do?"

"We're just part of it," I continued. "There are several more, most of our men fighting in the war are-"

"I don't want to hear it!" he shouted. "Do you realize your people have slaughtered thousands of my country's citizens? And not just soldiers. Their bombs rip through our cities and kill millions of people every day."

I closed my mouth, stunned. I knew the war was awful, but I had no idea the Mainframe had ordered such senseless killing. I floundered for something to say, but the words wouldn't come.

"You're now prisoners of war," he grunted. He commanded another sailor to take us to the brig. The man grabbed us roughly and dragged us farther down below decks to a cramped room. He shut the heavy door and bolted it into place.

Avery glared at me. "Way to go. Couldn't you see they were from Epirus?"

"I just saved your life," I shot back. "You could at least be thankful for that."

"Yeah, but your big mouth just made us prisoners of war."

I shrugged miserably and faced away from her. Hot tears sprang to my eyes, and I didn't bother to wipe them away. After all, she was right. We were trapped, and it was my fault.

Chapter Sixteen
Lily

"Well?" said Avery.

"Well what?"

"What are we going to do? We have to find a way out of here."

I rolled my eyes. "It's hopeless, Avery. They bolted the door."

She got up angrily and started looking around. "There's got to be a vent or something here."

"They know the ship in and out," I replied. "Even if we tried, they'd find us."

"Yeah, but they don't know we're armed," she said. She opened her jacket slyly to show a small pistol tucked into her belt. "I always carry this with me, just in case."

"It's wet, Avery," I replied. "I don't think it's going to fire now."

"It has a centrefire cartridge, duh! They're made to be waterproof."

"I'm sure they have guns too, and they'll be more than willing to use them. Besides, even if we did somehow make it up to deck, what would we do? Plunge overboard?"

"I overheard some guys talking about setting course for Kal. It's the capitol there, and it's not far from the border. We could wait until they're in port and make a dash for it."

"Avery, just drop it," I muttered. I rolled over onto my side and lay still, completely exhausted. She didn't say anything more, so for the moment I allowed myself to relax. Despite no blankets and an uncomfortable floor, I was soon fast asleep.

"Get up!"

I opened my eyes blearily and looked up into the stern face of an officer. He took us both by the arms, cuffed us and led us to the upper decks.

"We've reached port. You both will be heading to prison for questioning." We followed, but I wondered if Avery still had some kind of secret plan involving her gun. Given the circumstances in this country, gun violence probably wouldn't be the best way to get out of our predicament.

We marched down the gangplank onto a small pier. Soldiers and sailors alike bustled around, loading cargo onto ships, cleaning or tying down ropes.

I looked over at Avery, but she kept her eyes downcast. A new wave of fear crept over me as I realized we really had no hope of escape. So many people surrounded us that a break would be impossible.

We were shoved into a sleek, black car and driven a short distance to a plain, square building and shuffled inside to a small, windowless room.

"Wait here," grunted our captor as he shoved us into some chairs and left. I moved my hands, trying to alleviate the digging metal, but they only dug in deeper.

"What are we gonna do?" I muttered to Avery, who'd slumped over dejectedly. "You were all ready to go last night."

"Oh, now you suddenly want to escape?" she shot back. "You told me just to give up and give in."

"I didn't say that!"

"Yes, you did!"

I sighed impatiently. "Look, this isn't getting us anywhere. We need to come up with a plan."

"How can we? We're miles from the border, we have no one on our side because they think we're bloodthirsty savages and we're being held in a prison. With cuffs."

I leaned back against the wall and closed my eyes. A surge of frustration swept through me, giving me that familiar but nearly forgotten feeling of power.

I sat up. I'd completely forgotten about my hybridity, about my freak powers. I'd gotten out of scrapes with them before, why couldn't I now?

But my flare of hope died as I looked at Avery. If I used my ability to get us out, she'd discover me for sure. Even if we got out of here, I'd be dead.

A tall man suddenly burst through the door, his ruddy face bright under his dark hair. He stomped over to us and sat down across the desk.

"Names?" he barked, startling us both. Avery looked pointedly at me before rattling off some random name. He typed it into some kind of large data pad, then looked at me.

"Um…Sheryl Durham," I said.

He jerked us to our feet roughly and took each of our hands. Something cold and metal pressed against my finger.

"I'm taking your fingerprints. Our offices will tap the records in Illyria and double check your identities just in case you're using some kind of false identity."

He stomped out and slammed the door behind him. I looked at Avery, her face mirroring the worry I felt. Panic gripped me as I thought of what they'd do when they found out I was the capitol's most wanted criminal.

"They'll know we're lying," I whispered tensely. "I can't let them find out who I am."

She frowned at me. "What makes you so special?"

I bit my lip, cursing myself for my stupid slip. "I just mean we're both outlaws. They could put a huge ransom over our head and send us back to the Mainframe's mercy just to stop the war or something. We need to get out of here!"

I looked around the room frantically, trying to find anything that would help us, but the room lay bare except for a couple chairs. It was hardly a room, for that matter. More like a closet.

I looked at Avery and suddenly remembered her gun. If she could shoot the lock off, we might have a chance.

"Did they take your gun?"

She looked up at me. "No, but you yourself said it wouldn't be any use."

"Against these people, yeah, but couldn't you shoot the lock on the door?"

She turned so I could see the metal manacle binding her wrists. "Yeah, sure. One problem, though. I'm *cuffed*."

I sank back down in my chair, completely defeated. How could I have forgotten the cuffs with my wrists chafed and screaming in pain?

I looked determinedly at the door, not willing to give up. Maybe I could make myself angry over something and kick the door in. I definitely had plenty of reasons to be angry.

But before I could send myself into a blind rage, the building suddenly shook. Avery looked at me, panic once more etching her face. A low boom sounded somewhere and the building began to shake more violently. The chairs scattered across the room, looking like weird, fleeing animals.

"What's going on?" I called over the noise.

"I think it's a raid," Avery called back, her voice rising with fear.

Cold fear gripped me as I thought of bombs falling all around us. *Bombs from our own country.* I ran around the room uselessly, looking for an escape, until a particularly loud blast knocked me off my feet and across the room. I hit the wall and watched dazedly as starts popped before my eyes.

"Lily! The door!"

My blurred vision finally cleared. Avery stood looking at the door, which had busted from its hinges. I got up quickly and swayed a little, but a sudden surge of strength shot through me. I hobbled over to the door and pushed the outlying corner with my foot. It budged a little, making my heart leap. Avery nudged with her elbow until we finally moved the door enough to escape. We ducked through the low opening and glanced around. Thankfully, no one was around. Avery crept down the hall and I followed carefully, trying not to disturb the rubble. I could hear distant shouts and screams through the building, but most of the damage must have occurred on the other side because most of the hallway here was intact.

We rounded the corner and came to the hallway leading to the main lobby. People rushed around frantically trying to find a place to hide until the raid was done or helping the wounded who'd sustained injuries in the blast.

"What do we do now?" I whispered.

Avery didn't answer. She seemed to be scanning the crowd. Finally, she seemed to come to some decision.

"Follow me, and do exactly what I do," she whispered. She began to stagger unnaturally like some drunk. I followed suit, feeling ridiculous.

"No, not that way, it'll look dumb if we both have the same injury. My leg is broken. You've got a bruise on your head from bumping that wall. Pretend you have a concussion. If anyone says anything, act dumb."

I followed her, trying to make my eyes look glazed and disoriented. A woman with blonde hair who'd just bandaged a badly cut leg looked at us sharply.

"Aren't you the prisoners?" she asked as we hobbled through. She looked at me, and I swayed a little.

"The room collapsed," Avery gasped, playing the part of leg victim well. "We had to crawl through the wreckage of the door before the room collapsed on us. We would have died if we'd stayed in there."

"Serves you right," she snapped. "Just get out of my way, I have work to do."

"Please, ma'am, we're not spies. We just wound up in the wrong place at the wrong time," Avery pleaded. "My leg is broken and I think my friend has a concussion."

A few tears fell from her eyes as a realistic sob escaped her throat. I tried not to show how much she'd impressed me with her acting. The woman's hard stare faltered for just a second.

"I don't help you people," she muttered. "All you've done is tear our country apart."

"I know," Avery replied with a wince. "You have to understand, though, we have no control either. We swam into the ocean to get away from things going on in Illyria and nearly drowned. If your country's patrol ship hadn't saved us, we'd be dead. We don't mean any harm to anyone. My leg hurts terribly and all I want is a splint and a head bandage for my friend."

As if on cue, a small trickle of blood made its way down my face from the bruised cut I'd gotten in the blast. I closed my eyes in mock pain.

The woman tightened her lips, looking around nervously as if expecting someone to jump out. Finally, her shoulders slumped in resignation.

"Ok, I'll help. But stay quiet and out of the way when I'm through."

She rushed off and came back with some bandages and a long piece of plastic. Deftly, she aligned the piece on Avery's leg and wound it securely with a bandage. Then she turned to me and wound another bandage gently around my head.

"Thank you very much," Avery whispered. The woman looked at her for a second, her eyes softened and sad.

"You really are innocent, aren't you?" she asked in a low voice.

Avery merely nodded. "But I don't blame you if you don't believe us."

The woman looked around nervously again. "Listen...I know I shouldn't do this, but I can't just ignore what I know is wrong. I know I could be making the stupidest mistake of my life, but I've heard things from your soldiers about what it's like in Illyria and...well...no one should have to go through that. I'm not saying what they're doing is right, but I don't think they have much choice."

"They don't," I blurted out. I bit my lip as Avery glared at me, but the woman gave a slight nod as if to say she understood.

She pulled an electronic key from her pocket and inserted it into the small locks on our cuffs. The metal bands retracted into their coils as the woman shoved them back into her pocket. She began to walk away briskly, clearly scared, but then stopped. She turned and walked quickly back to us.

"Listen, if you're smart, you'll leave before the warden gets back," she whispered. "Get out the door, to the right and open the side gate. Everyone is trying to recover from this blast, so you'll have time."

She looked at Avery. "I'm sorry I don't have a crutch for you, but maybe it's better if you don't run. It'll look suspicious. That splint should hold."

"Thank you," Avery repeated. "I can't tell you how much you've helped."

The woman just nodded, turned and left. Avery grabbed my arm in a vice grip and steered me toward the door. We looked carefully around, then crept through it to the courtyard outside.

The scenes outside made my stomach turn. Smoke filled the air, rising from the ruins of what used to be large city buildings. People stumbled around coughing and crying, trying to clear wreckage or calling for help. Avery yanked me down the along the wall to the right until we came to the side gate, just as the woman described. We didn't even have to open it. Huge holes had been blown through the mesh fencing. It was easy enough to crawl through them into an alley next to a huge skyscraper.

A loud blast suddenly sounded behind us. I looked back to see a skyscraper tumble down as if it were made of sand. My ears rang oddly and I was vaguely aware that Avery pulled on my arm. I looked back at her and saw her lips form the word "Move."

I staggered with her through the wreckage strewn streets, my heart seized with terror. I couldn't figure out how the bombs had come so noiselessly until I remembered learning about the Invisi-Jets the Mainframe created a few years back. Military history was required in school even though it was pretty much everyone's most hated subject. The planes could swoop in noiselessly, invisibly, and wreak havoc without ever being detected.

As if a flip switched, my hearing suddenly came back. Screams filled the air, coupled with the wail of sirens. I almost wished I was deaf again.

As we came to an open square in the city, a group of Rovers came through the surrounding alleys. Soldiers poured out of them, knocking down everyone and everything in their path. Avery yanked me down another side alley, away from the mayhem, when a lone soldier caught my eye. He stood back away from the others, a hard, fearful spite marring his once sun-tanned face and poisoning his hazel eyes. Those hazel eyes I'd stared into so many times. His arms and hands, the ones that once held me so protectively, now cradled a massive gun. I watched in horror as thousands of blue-uniformed soldiers appeared from nowhere, picking off the Illyrian soldiers one by one. The man crumpled to the ground as the bullet found its target.

I stumbled towards him, my head in total disarray, my heart rising in my throat.

"*Wes!*"

Chapter Seventeen
Lily

"Are you *crazy*??" Avery hissed. She grabbed my arm roughly and yanked me back into the shadowy alley. "We need to get as far away from the city as possible!"

"But…" I glanced back at Wes, only to discover it wasn't him after all. This man looked similar, but was slightly taller. His hair was shaggy like Wes's, but the color was different. I tried to rid myself of my shock, reminding myself over and over that Wes was alive, but I still felt shock.

Avery dragged me down the alley away from the battle. Shouts, screams, gunfire and loud, booming blasts filled the air until I thought my head would explode from the din. A hazy smoke filled the air, making me pull up my shirt around my nose. My eyes stung as I hurried after Avery, trying to find our way.

Suddenly, she stopped and I looked to where she stared. A sleek, dark gray car had been abandoned across the street, the driver and passenger door slid open, the keycard still in the ignition. We looked at each other, thinking the same thing at the same time. In one swift movement, we rushed to the car and jumped in. The doors slid agonizingly slowly until they finally closed with a satisfying click. Avery programmed the engine and swung around to face the other way. We shot through the streets, neatly avoiding small craters, fallen debris and terrified citizens rushing through the streets and alleys. Using the digital compass, Avery kept a northern course.

At last, we reached a more open route leading out of the city. A blockade had been set up, but Avery deftly circled it and shot ahead. A few men shouted and scrambled into patrol cars, but Avery took a side street to the east, followed by several more winding passages, until we wound up on a lone road surrounded by steep mountains. The patrol would have had no time to catch up. I realized with a start we'd already made it to the small mountain range that sat on the border with Illyria.

Avery relaxed a little and leaned back in her seat. "Close one," she breathed.

I nodded, still a little too adrenaline-hyped to answer. I thought again of the man who'd looked so much like Wes. The familiar ache crept into my heart again, threatening to overwhelm me. I thought back to the last time I'd seen him, those last moments on the beach. I tried to calculate how much time had passed, and figured about two weeks. How could it have been so short? It felt as if it had been months ago.

A single tear traced my cheek. I wiped it quickly so Avery wouldn't see. He'd done so much to protect me. I let out a quiet sigh of frustration. The horrible carnage we'd seen in the Epirian capitol made my stomach churn. I'd known the war was bad, but I hadn't known it was a slaughter. The man on the ship was right. Our soldiers had become senseless killers, and I could do nothing to help Wes.

I closed my eyes, holding back the tears. For whatever reason, Avery sensed not to pester me with questions and stayed quiet.

"You've gotta be kidding me," she muttered darkly a while later. We'd been driving down the narrow pass through the mountains at terrific speed, but she tapped the screen quickly, trying to decelerate. I looked ahead and felt my stomach drop. Ahead stood a fortress-like tower surrounded by mesh fencing. The border. We'd completely forgotten about the border.

Without warning, Avery slowed completely to a stop quite a distance from the tower. She concentrated hard, muttering to herself and tapping her fingers on the wheel.

"We'll never get through," she said aloud. "We'll be shot the minute we try to go through."

"Why? Don't people cross all the time?"

"Not in a war, Lily. Their side will brand us spies and have us shot, no question. Our side will think we're southerners. We can't risk it."

I shrugged. "Use your gun. Shoot them first."

She glared at me. "Is that all you think I am? A killing machine?"

"What? You talked about using it on the ship."

She clenched her fists around the wheel. "Yeah, as a threat, not to actually kill anyone." Her face darkened as she looked ahead. "I only shoot beasts that can't help themselves. It's actually helping them by putting them out of their misery."

"Ok, ok, I get it!" I snapped. "We need to do something before they wonder why there's a random car parked in the middle of nowhere."

Without replying, she shifted into neutral and guided the car slowly to the edge of the road.

"Get out," she ordered tersely.

We crept quietly out of the car and covered it with nearby shrubbery at her command. "There. Hopefully it'll take a while for anyone to find it."

The low rumble of an engine sounded nearby. Avery and I darted up into the foothills and crouched behind some scrubby underbrush. A black car with shadowed windows drove slowly along the road to the border. I wondered for a moment if someone had followed us, then shook the thought. No one knew where we'd gone.

After the car drove out of sight, Avery motioned me to follow her. We climbed higher through the mountains to the opposite side where we couldn't be found. The sun descended lower towards the horizon, making me nervous. I didn't have much experience in the wilderness, but I knew being out alone and exposed at night wasn't a good idea. The hot air pressed down on me, the heavy cotton uniforms we'd received on the ship making beads of sweat run down my back.

Avery eventually spotted a small cave. We trekked through the brush towards it and managed to find a small stream nearby. It had been so long without water for both of us that we drank for a while. Avery looked up at the sun and hurried off.

"Stay here, I'll get some food."

I leaned against the side of the cave, realizing for the first time how tired I really was. The ground felt cool beneath me, alleviating some of the intense heat radiating from my skin. I laid back against the rough wall, found a comfortable spot, and dozed.

I woke a while later, my skin covered in goose bumps. The air had grown quite a bit colder, though I knew we were still in the summer months. I remembered then that mountains could get cold at night, even in the height of summer, and groaned. The cotton shirt and pants felt so heavy earlier, but now they felt skimpy against my freezing skin.

I looked up into the sky, startled to see a high, full moon and a scattering of stars. I didn't have a watch, but I knew several hours had passed. I looked around, expecting to see Avery. Maybe she hadn't woken me up because she hadn't found anything.

I couldn't see her, so I got up and slowly crept around the cave. I even called her name softly a few times, with no response.

Panic rose in my throat. Had she been caught? I looked around and shook the thought. We'd hiked into a small valley created by several small mountains. The road we'd traveled was remote, definitely not the main route. No one would find us.

And yet, something was wrong. My heart thumped irregularly as I considered that she might have found a lot of food and had to carry it back in shifts.

With this small comfort, I folded my arms inside my t-shirt to stay warm and waited. The night grew colder as a slight breeze picked up. I huddled my knees to my chest and scanned the view from one mountain on my right to another on my left.

Hours and hours of waiting still didn't reveal Avery. I jumped at every rustle of leaves, every animal call, until I thought I'd lose it. As the sky lightened to a dark grey and the stars began to disappear, I knew without a doubt she was in trouble. I got up, rubbed my cold, aching limbs and walked around to warm up.

"Come on, Avery," I whispered. "Please, come back."

Pink streaks crossed the sky, the precursor of dawn. I bit my nails down into the nubs, still scanning, still watching. Nothing.

With no other choice, I started off down the path she'd taken, anxious to find her, but also scared of what I might find.

Chapter Eighteen
Wes

The soldier stared at Wes, his eyes full of hate. The trapped man tried to lunge at him, but the Epirian men held him back.

"You two know each other?" said the Epirian doctor, looking at Wes. He took a deep breath, trying to figure out what to do.

"He's a low-down, scummy traitor, that's what he is," spat the prisoner, still glaring at Wes. The other Epirian man took a step towards Wes, surprise and anger filling his eyes.

"You're Illyrian?" he asked, obviously trying to keep his voice steady. "Why aren't you in confinement?"

Wes held up his hands in mock surrender. "Look, I'll talk, I swear. I don't want to hurt anyone. I've spent the whole day here taking care of the wounded. I don't agree with what the government's doing, I swear. I think it's horrible."

He shook his head angrily and started towards Wes. "I don't care what you say, if you're a northerner, you're no good."

He grabbed Wes's arm roughly, then drew back as if he'd been burned, his face a mask of revulsion. "What's wrong with your arm?"

Wes looked to where he pointed. He didn't have his jacket on, leaving his arm with the bulging tracker exposed.

"What is that?" the foreign man asked, pointing to the bulging lump.

"It's…a tracker-" Wes started, but the doctor cut him off.

"You some kind of spy?" he shouted, looking slightly panicked now.

"No, I swear, I…"

The doctor pulled out a small communicator and barked into it for more backup. Wes gave up trying to explain anything, realizing no one would bother to listen to him now that they knew who he was.

Two heavily armed men came through the front set of doors and talked in whispers to the man who'd called them. The doctor pointed towards Wes, and the two burly guards dragged him from the room, through the doors into the smoky air outside. They led him to a small car with dark windows and shoved him in. Wes slumped against the seat, defeated and exhausted. He didn't even bother to look outside at the passing landscape this time as the car drove on and on. From what he gathered from the two men in the front seat, they'd have gotten to their destination sooner if the car hadn't had to take so many detours around debris.

Wes fell asleep along the way, and woke suddenly when the car jerked abruptly to a stop. He sat up and rubbed his eyes, knowing immediately something was wrong. His two captors had jumped suddenly from the car and unslung their guns. Wes crept to the window and looked out. The guards had crouched behind some debris and aimed their guns at someone. Two soldiers in green dashed out from among some buildings, but one fell suddenly, the victim of a well-aimed shot. Other uniformed soldiers darted among the rubble. Wes then realized that the Invisi-Jets must have dropped soldiers in on parachute in an attempt to overtake the capitol by ground forces.

He sat back against the seat, trying to decide what to do. He figured he could jump out and fight, but worried about having nothing to fight with. The men had unfortunately remembered to take the keys with them, so he had no way of driving away and escaping.

He looked out the window again, noting that the street now lay littered with blue-uniformed soldiers, twisting and convulsing in strange ways. The Illyrian soldiers wore masks of some kind as they raided a nearby food storage center. The men who'd left the car now came rushing back, looks of terror on their faces. They jumped into the car and roared off, clearly terrified.

"They've never used anything like that before," said one of the men, out of breath.

"We've gotta get to HQ," said the other. "We don't have anything to fight hallucinogenic gas."

Wes sat stunned, and slightly unbelieving. *Gas*? On human beings? He felt a sickening surge of disgust at the new lows the Mainframe had swept to. The man in the passenger seat shot a dirty look back at Wes.

"Like what your fellow men are doing?" he sneered. "We'll talk to the chief as soon as you're taken care of."

In a short time, they pulled up to a large building atop a hill. The massive size and grandeur of the building gave it away immediately as the main government building. Wes thought wryly that they could have been a little less conspicuous, but then realized they probably hadn't bargained on war.

The car pulled to a stop directly in front of the building. The men shoved Wes roughly to his feet, each securing a strong hand around his arms. They led him through the doors into a main lobby, then down a side hall to a dark, windowless room. The building, though grand, wasn't nearly as lavishly furnished as the Mainframe had been.

Wes sat down at a desk while the men left him and bolted the door behind them. With nothing else to do, he propped his feet up on the desk and leaned back, glad to sit down again. The sandwiches at the hospital seemed ages ago now, and the lack of food and sleep had made him very weak and tired.

After what felt like ages, he heard arguing outside the door. Two men shouted loudly at each other, not bothering to keep their voices down. Wes strained his ears as much as he could, but he couldn't quite make out what they were saying.

The door burst open, and he felt hope rising within him once more. Conley, the man who'd asked him to help at the hospital, strode in, looking angry.

"There you are! I needed your help, and these idiots carted you off!"

Wes smiled in spite of the situation. Conley had to know what had happened, but he still seemed to be on Wes's side.

"He's a spy, he has a tracker," shouted the other man, the one who'd given Wes the look in the vehicle on the way to the building.

"Use your brain, Hensley," Conley barked. "Why would he willingly help us in the hospital when the creeps up north probably gave him access to every horrible weapon they've got? I know you think just because their government is hideous that all of them are that way, but a lot of the soldiers I've met have resisted their orders."

"But…but…" the man spluttered indignantly. "Look at his arm!"

Wes held his arm out willingly. "It is a tracker. He's right," Wes explained wearily. "They put it on me to track me, not to find a way here. I'm on a special assignment, and they want to make sure it gets done."

Conley sat down. "What's your assignment? If you talk, we'll go easier on you."

The other man, Hensley, rolled his eyes angrily and crossed his arms. Wes looked back at Conley, hoping against hope he would say the right thing.

"I'm supposed to find a person," Wes replied. "She has…a weapon that they need. If I don't do it in the next eight days or so, the tracker will inject poison into my bloodstream and kill me."

The other guard across from him raised his eyebrows skeptically. "Why would they kill one of their soldiers off?"

"They've wanted this person for a long time, but she keeps getting away. They did it as an incentive for me to find her faster."

"What has she got that they want so bad?" asked Hensley in a cruel voice. "Since when do girls even know how to use weapons?"

Wes tried to hide his irritation as he looked at the man. "It's…a long story," Wes replied finally.

"We've got all the time in the world," said Conley.

Wes shrugged. "Ok…"

For the next half hour, he explained about Lily's strange gift, her seeming immunity to the effects of the Akrium. The Epirian soldiers looked steadily more skeptical as Wes talked. When he finished, Hensley crossed his arms and shot an "I told you so" look at Conley.

"Well," said Conley, "I suppose you know what we need to do now."

Wes nodded glumly, not caring what happened anymore. All he really wanted was to sleep.

"We've got to cut the tracker out."

Chapter Nineteen
Wes

Wes stared at Conley, stunned. The soldier doctor stood up and paced the room, rubbing his chin thoughtfully.

"Listen, I don't know what it is, but I think you're telling the truth," he said. "I don't see why a guy working for the other side would help us. You've had every opportunity to kill us and you haven't."

"He's obviously a spy!" spluttered Hensley.

"Then that's all the more reason to cut out the tracker," replied Conley. "Even if it's a tracker to help the cretins up north, if we tear it out, we'll ruin their plans. And if he's telling the truth, he won't go find this super girl they want so bad. Either way, it's win win."

Wes's heart sank a little. He had no plans to do what the Mainframe told him, but he wanted badly to find Lily anyway.

"And what are you going to do with him when we're done? Let him run free and go spying back to Illyria?"

"No. We'll put him to work in border patrol. The guys up there are short anyway, and going crazy because of it."

Wes had no idea what that meant, but he didn't dare say anything more. The men seemed to be letting him off, along with entrusting him to some kind of patrol.

Hensley left the room, cursing under his breath. Wes looked up at Conley, who wore a half smile across his broad face.

"Thanks," Wes said, feeling like an idiot but not knowing how else to show his appreciation. He let out a sigh of relief, knowing he was off the hook.

"You're welcome," he replied. "Just help us win this war, ok?"

Wes nodded, feeling slightly conflicted at the prospect of fighting his native country, but too tired to really care. Wes followed Conley through the door, down the hall and back out to another waiting car. He sat in the back once more as Conley drove, another man in the front seat. Drowsiness overtook Wes again, and it seemed as if they pulled up to the hospital in a matter of minutes.

Wes was led through the doors again and taken to the wing next to the one he'd previously worked in. The men led him to a bed, explaining that they didn't have any surgeons on hand right then, but would in the morning. Wes just nodded wearily and dropped into the bed, passing out as soon as his head hit the pillow.

Bright sunlight woke Wes the next morning, though he felt slightly cold. He looked over at a nearby electronic calendar and noticed with a jolt that it was late August. He sat up, every limb in his body aching from the effort. He looked at his arm, expecting to see some kind of huge scar, but the large bump remained. Panic suddenly overtook him as he wondered how long he'd been out, how long the tracker had been in his arm.

Just then, Conley walked in and smiled broadly. "I know, I know, but we wanted to let you sleep. We've been keeping track, and the thing in your arm needs to come out soon, but it won't kill you yet. We've got a surgeon already lined up."

Wes raised his eyebrows skeptically. "How do I know this isn't a trick?"

"Hey, we could have killed you in your sleep, couldn't we?" He laughed and shook his head. "As long as you scratch our backs, we'll scratch yours."

Wes relaxed and leaned back against the scratchy hospital pillows. He had no other way to put it-Conley looked a little scary. His dark, graying hair protruded over his hardened brow, a brow that must have been accustomed to frowning. Only his eyes, pale blue and happy, betrayed his kindness. They sat nestled beneath huge, caterpillar-like brows, and his mouth usually sat in a tight line. But Wes had never met anyone so friendly, so…positive.

After an outstanding breakfast of ham and eggs, a doctor came in who couldn't have been much older than Wes. He stared at the doctor nervously.

"I know what you're thinking," the man said casually as he pulled on rubber gloves. "But I've operated on a number of people, and only a few have died on my watch."

He grinned, but Wes didn't see the humor given the fact that people were dying in droves every day, but he kept his mouth shut. The doctor injected Wes slowly with some kind of clear liquid that instantly made him drowsy. He fell back against the pillows into darkness. Out of nowhere, Lily's face suddenly loomed before him, her haunting green eyes staring intensely into mine. Wes tried to reach out and touch her, but couldn't. The darkness pulled him under again, suffocating him with its power.

When he woke, Wes struggled to lift his eyelids. His arms felt as if they'd been puttied with lead and his head ached. Incoherent voices swirled around him, making no sense. Wes wished more than anything that he could fall back into the blackness and see her face again, but he felt himself gradually rising through the layers of confusion.

"He's coming round," someone said. Wes opened his eyes to see Conley and the doctor hovering above him, probably waiting to see his reaction.

"How'd it go?" Wes asked, his voice muffled and thick. Though his body still tried to push him under the spell of the painkillers, his brain stayed alert, now taking in all the surroundings. The windows showed twilight rather than the early morning sunlight he'd remembered.

"We had a few…complications," said the doctor hesitantly. "That's why it took so long. But don't worry, we got you fixed up in the end."

"What happened?" Wes nearly shouted, sitting up in bed. "I knew you didn't know what you were doing!" He looked down at his arm, surprised to see a neat seam with sealant over it to heal the skin. The bump from the tracker was no longer visible.

"Listen," the doctor replied, "I'm sorry. I didn't quite realize how the tracker worked. I had no problems with the surgery part, but the tracker released some poison before we could fully get it out. I think it was rigged to do that, in case you tried to cut it out yourself."

"Oh," Wes replied, feeling dumb.

"The poison was localized, thankfully, but we had to clean it, seal you up quick and get some antidotes pumped into you before the poison took effect. We used about ten different kinds of antidotes before we finally got the right one, since it was a pretty tricky poison. You had some convulsions and your heart rate dropped a couple times. But you're here."

"Thanks," Wes replied slowly, feeling even more stupid for criticizing a man who'd just saved his life. He looked up at the men searchingly.

"Why would you do this for me?" he asked. Conley looked at the doctor and shrugged.

"We trust you."

"That's it? You trust me?"

"All you've done is help us," Conley said. "So, we figured we owed you one. Besides, it doesn't hurt to have an ex-patriot on our side."

"Well...ok. Thanks."

"We're going to keep you here for observation for another day, then get you set up as a patrol guard," said the doctor. "It's fairly easy, since Illyrians always come by boat or air, but it'll still help us out a good deal."

"Fine with me," Wes replied. He thought of Lily again and sighed inwardly. In Vic's twisted plan, he realized he might have at least seen her one last time before the poison killed him, but now he didn't know if he'd ever see her again. It plagued him not knowing what happened to her, but he comforted himself with the thought that the border post would be a good place to keep an eye out for her. He knew she was still evading capture, otherwise it would have been very publicly televised.

As Wes showered and ate some lunch later on, a few people rushed through the hallway outside his wing, talking loudly and excitedly.

"More spies! Girls this time, and trying to talk their way out of it, but they came in on a freighter. Lost in the ocean."

"Why'd they pick 'em up in the first place?" said another loud voice.

"Because they didn't know they were Illyrians at the time, stupid. Anyway, we gotta get over there, there are wounded people from the last blast."

Wes sat up, his heart pounding. The draft, as it had for so long, excluded girls, so they could easily be random girls. Still...something nagged at me. One of them might be Lily. It would make sense for her to try and escape by sea. Maybe she'd found some way to hire a dingy or something, he realized, and it had shipwrecked.

"Where are they at?" asked the other voice, still carrying on loudly, sounding as if the person were out of breath.

"The prison. They're gonna be hauled in for questioning, no doubt," the other replied. Their voices slowly faded down the hall. Wes jumped out of bed and ran out of the room, trying to find Conley. Luckily, he strode down the hall towards his room at that very moment.

"Conley! Those two guys mentioned something about prisoners found in the ocean. Do you know their names?"

He scratched his head. "No…why do you need to know?"

"Because I think I know one of them, and she's in danger. I need to get to her, fast!"

He grinned. "Girlfriend?"

Wes let out an exasperated growl. "Yeah, she's my girlfriend, but she is in danger. She's the one I told you about."

Conley sobered at once. "Get to the lobby. I'll meet you in fifteen minutes with a car."

Chapter Twenty
Wes

Wes and Conley rushed out to the car and jumped in. Conley pushed his foot all the way down on the gas pedal, making the car shoot down the road at lightning speed. Again, the two wound through dizzying scenes of destruction, the car weaving to avoid the large potholes and wreckage that dotted the road.

Suddenly, the all too familiar hum sounded overhead. Wes looked at Conley, whose face had paled with terror.

"Perfect timing," he muttered sarcastically. A loud, shuddering boom sounded loudly across the city block, and for a moment Wes couldn't hear anything. Conley screamed as a huge chunk of something flew straight at the windshield. He yanked the wheel hard to the right, ramming the car straight into a city building.

As Wes's hearing slowly came back, he looked around dazedly and saw Conley by his side, shouting as loud as he could. He blinked, trying to make sense of the loud muddle of words, but nothing came.

"I can't hear you!" he shouted, feeling odd that he could barely hear himself.

"What?" Conley said, his lips forming around the familiar word. Wes held his hand up to his ear and shrugged. Conley cursed, then turned to his door and tried to shake it loose. It had been jammed in the collision. He turned towards Wes again and motioned towards the opposite door. Wes tried it, but it wouldn't budge. All the electrical wires controlling the door slide had been mangled in the crash. Wes looked up and noticed a moon roof. It was electronic too, but he wondered if they might be able to break it. He searched the car for anything heavy, but couldn't find anything. Desperately, he took off a boot and shouted to Conley to get his boots too. He slammed the massive combat boot against the heavy glass with no luck. Conley followed suit, slamming his boot against the glass, until finally it began to crack slightly.

With one last grunt of effort, Wes slammed as hard as he could against the glass and it cracked completely. The outer coating finally gave, and the two men worked together to push through it. Wes allowed Conley to climb out first, then pushed himself up as Conley helped him out. Some of Wes's hearing had finally come back, so he could hear himself thanking Conley.

"How close are we?" Wes panted, trying to catch his breath, having lost it from shock and adrenaline.

Conley looked around. "We're on Carlisle avenue...I'd say twenty minutes walking."

They jumped down from the car and started running, the wreckage and screaming survivors passing in a frightening blur. Before they'd gotten ten steps, however, another shuddering blast knocked them off their feet. The air was now filled with so much noxious gas that the two could barely breathe. Wes struggled to his feet and helped Conley up, noticing with dismay that he'd cut his arm pretty bad in the fall. The gash hung open, raw red and infectious. Wes ripped off part of his dirty shirt and wrapped it hastily around the wound.

Other people around them screamed and cried, some struggling to their feet while others stayed alarmingly still. Conley and Wes rushed around, trying to help as best they could. Wes wanted to help these people in any way he could, but he got more and more uneasy as the minutes ticked by. Lily was in the city. He knew where she might be, and yet he couldn't get to her.

At long last, an ambulance showed up and some familiar comrades from the hospital jumped out and rushed to the aid of the victims. They cleaned and bandaged Conley more professionally and begged his help, but he shook his head. Wes looked at him gratefully, silently hurrying him on.

"We're on other business, but I'll be there as soon as I can," he replied. "Let's go," he said to Wes. They ran through the complex maze of rubble and victims, turning at last onto a large thoroughfare where traffic sat at a standstill.

The two friends finally approached another unfamiliar building that stood tall and imposing against the sky. As they rushed inside, Wes noticed pockmarks on the building, evidence of the recent blast. This had to be some kind of main headquarters since the bomb blasts had come so close.

The main lobby was in chaos as we pushed through the doors. People rushed around, frightened, but none of them looked like Lily. Pushing through the terror-struck crowds, they ran up the stairs and through as many levels as they could. Most of the rooms were simple offices filled with cubicles, but one hallway on the third floor held a room with no windows. The door had been shaken loose by the blast. Eagerly, Wes peeked inside.

"They there?" Conley asked.

He climbed inside for a better look. Nothing but chairs and a small table. He busted the door off completely, looked around and shook his head.

"No. Something must've happened. Let's head back to the lobby and ask around."

They started down the stairs again, navigating once more through terrified groups of people. When they finally got to the lobby, the crowd had thinned considerably. A blonde woman rushed around helping victims who couldn't move. Wes ran to her, figuring if anyone was in charge here, it would be her.

"Ma'am, what happened to the prisoners?" he asked, hoping to catch her off guard. She looked up, startled, then settled her face back into a look of surprise.

"You mean they're not in the interrogation room?"

Wes could tell immediately that she was lying. "We *have* to find them. Do you know anything?"

She avoided his eyes carefully. "No. I've just been taking care of patients."

"You don't understand, this is life or death," Wes replied, trying to keep his voice even. "Did you see them?"

"I don't know what you're talking about," she snapped. "If you don't mind, I'm trying to care for these people until medics arrive. Excuse me."

With that, she walked off. Wes glanced at Conley, who shrugged. "Sorry, man."

Wes shook his head. "It's not your fault."

It took all of Wes's restraint to stop himself from punching the wall. She'd been here, he knew she had, and that woman definitely knew something. Not that he could blame her. If he'd helped the enemy in a war zone, he realized he probably wouldn't want anyone to know, either.

Conley clapped Wes on the back understandingly. "We'll find her," he said, attempting a smile.

Wes appreciated Conley's effort to cheer him up, but he couldn't ignore the terror rising in his heart. Lily had been so close, and he'd lost her again.

Chapter Twenty-One
Lily

The air grew steadily warmer the farther I ventured into the valley. The sun finally began to rise in earnest, peeking over the tops of the mountains, the rays of light tumbling down to meet me. Though my heart still ached with worry for Avery, I realized that for the first time since I'd found Wes up north, I felt peace. I'd known noise and chaos for most of my life, so the clean mountain air and soft breeze were a pleasant change.

For nearly an hour, I hiked among the trees and hills, scanning intently for any sign of Avery without results. As the sun climbed higher in the sky, I took my arms out of the thick cotton shirt. Sweat made the material cling to my back unrelentingly until I was forced to find shade. A stream ran nearby, but my rumbling stomach grew louder. I found several berries and nuts, but held back. Avery's knowledge of plants and edible wild things far outweighed my own. What if these were poisonous?

I decided on some of the red berries and left the rest, praying that they weren't poisonous. After a short rest, I started across the rough landscape again, no longer appreciating the fresh breeze or the peace and quiet. As the hours passed, desperation grew inside me to the point where I nearly felt choked.

I stopped on a small outlook as the sun reached its apex, squinting against the light to find any sign of Avery. The outlook jutted out over a small, sloping cliff, reaching maybe fifteen to twenty feet down before it leveled out.

Suddenly, I noticed with a stab of fear a thick, torn, white piece of cotton resting on a tree. I climbed carefully down the steep mountainside, digging my muddy shoes into the soft dirt to make footholds for myself. As I reached the tree, I noticed with alarm a few bloodstains against the white.

I compared the material to mine. An exact match. My heart sinking, I stumbled into the surrounding trees.

"Avery!" I hollered. No answer.

"AVERY!"

I froze as an indistinct cry rose faintly through the trees. I stopped and strained my ears. "Lily?"

I ran haltingly, trying to go fast over the uneven terrain. I paused every few seconds as the call was repeated and altered course. Finally, I stumbled into a clearing to see Avery lying on the forest floor against a tree, her ankle swollen to nearly twice its size. A cut full of dried, crusty blood ran half the length of her calf.

"Oh, Lily, I'm so glad you finally came!" Her voice could barely go above a whisper, and her face had become alarmingly ashen. Her shirt and pants were bloody and torn. "I've been calling for hours."

My heart thumped hard as I moved closer and looked over her wound. "Wh-what happened?" My voice shook with a combination of shortness of breath and terror.

"It was dark, I was stupid…I shouldn't have gone looking at night, but I knew we were both starving. I took a misstep and fell down into this valley. I heard animals prowling, so I had to drag myself into the trees so I wasn't exposed."

She looked about ready to faint. I had no idea how to help, or even if I should move her. "Avery, you've got to help me, I don't know what to do."

"I need some clean cloth wrapped around this ankle. I tried to do it myself, but my hands were shaking too bad and I couldn't see."

I tore some cloth from the bottom of my pants and wrapped the ankle as best as I could with repeated instructions from Avery. A little color returned to her face, but I knew her pain was still intense.

"What else can I do?"

"See if you can find a willow tree with white, pointed leaves that grow downward along the stem," she murmured. "Cut a chunk of bark from it and bring it here."

I hurried off, using the trail marking tricks Avery had shown me, and looked carefully at all the trees. All of them seemed to be pine. I found a few evergreens, but the leaves didn't match what Avery was talking about. I wandered around for about twenty minutes before I finally found a tree near a small stream with leaves that grew in that particular pattern. Sure enough, the underside of the leaves was a distinctive white color. I grabbed a sharp rock and dug into the bark. After I got a few good size chunks, I hurried back along my path and luckily found Avery within a few minutes.

"Is this right?"

I held it out to her and she nodded. "Crush it up as best you can and mix it with some water. There's a stream not far from here."

I ran back to the stream I'd found near the tree. After finding a flat rock to pound on and a good size stone to crush the bark, I found a big leaf and cupped the water into it. The crushed bark mixed well. I carried it carefully back to Avery and let her drink.

"Is that any better?" I asked.

Avery closed her eyes. "Yeah, thank you. I think now I just need some sleep."

I gathered a bunch of pine needles into a pile in sort of a bed. Avery explained which berries and other things could be eaten, then snuggled in the bed of pines and drifted off. I wandered around the small clearing and found a few lumpy red berries that Avery called raspberries. Their sweet tartness surprised me as the thin berry skin burst in my mouth. I scavenged the whole bush, looking for more of the delicious berries, checking my hunger just in time to save a good amount for Avery to eat when she woke up. I gathered some small pine nuts as well, but a handful barely satisfied my hunger. After I'd eaten enough to satisfy my hunger, I managed to gather quite a few berries and nuts into a large leaf that I put beside Avery.

Fatigue suddenly washed over me, bringing me to my knees. I laid down in the soft, pungent dirt and instantly fell asleep.

After a while I felt myself falling, falling and landing gently in the middle of the large intersection in the capitol city of Epirus. A group of soldiers marched forward, guns raised, looking to kill. I hunched down, afraid they'd seen me, but they passed over me as if I were nothing more than a shadow. I sat up and looked around.

Terror choked me as I watched the men close in on Wes, their target. He stood alone in the center of the block, gun lying on the ground at his side. He stared boldly at the men, unafraid, unflinching. I rushed to him. He saw me, smiled, then crumpled as the bullets found their target.

"NO!"

Gunfire roared all around me, blending with the screams and shouts of the people of the city. I cowered, knowing they'd seen me, knowing I'd be discovered, waiting for the bullets to pierce me as they'd pierced Wes.

I sat up panting, confused, and looked around wildly. The soldiers, the guns, the city were gone. I sat in the forest in the little clearing where I'd found Avery. My breathing finally slowed, but something still wasn't right. The screams in my dream hadn't stopped. I ducked warily, wondering who could possibly be here, but no one was in sight. I looked over at Avery, but she lay motionless, apparently still sound asleep. I knew I'd heard *something*.

My eyes wandered to a patch of moonlight and my heart stopped. A giant, cat-like thing stood in the light, flicking its tail.

"Avery," I hissed. "Avery!"

I scooted slowly over to where she lay and shook her gently. Finally, she roused.

"What's-" she started, but I pressed my hand firmly against her mouth with one hand and pointed with the other. Her eyes grew wide.

Gently, she took my hand away from her face and looked up at me. "It's a cougar. A mountain lion. The ones I was telling you about."

I racked my brain, trying to figure out what she meant, when I remembered the eerie screams we'd heard in the Shadowlands.

"What do we do?" I whispered, trying to hear my own words over the frantic pace of my heart.

"Don't move."

We sat there in a perpetual staring contest with the creature. It began to walk first one way, then the other, never taking its eyes from us. In this zig-zag, it came closer and closer to us.

"Avery, do these things attack people?" I whispered.

"I don't know. I just know they sound like screaming women."

We lay there, rigid with fear, neither of us sure of what to do. The cougar came closer until I could reach my hand out and touch it. It opened its large jaws and gave another unearthly scream before it reared back and jumped.

Without warning, a low growl escaped my throat. The beast went straight for Avery, but my supernatural strength began to flow within me. I caught the animal by the claw and threw it off balance enough to keep it from getting to her. It growled and lunged at me instead, but I was ready. Instead of fighting against the movement of the animal, I caught him up and let him arch over me. The giant cat landed in a heap, but got to its feet in a moment and made ready to pounce.

Searching around, I finally found a long stick that looked as if it had been broken off a tree at an odd angle, giving it a sharp edge. I struck out at the cougar, making it back off just a little. It lunged again, jumping straight at me with claws extended. I plunged the stick into its heart and pushed back against the movement this time. Angrily, the creature swiped and got me on the wrists, but it seemed to know it lost. It flew back, its head cocked at an odd angle, before landing on the forest floor. The animal lay motionless, the stick still protruding from its chest.

I took a few deep breaths, trying to calm the massive adrenaline surging through my veins. Though I knew it only took a few minutes to kill the cougar, it felt as if everything had slowed down.

I finally looked up at Avery, expecting to see shock or surprise at the very least. The last thing I thought I'd see, though, was an expression of mingled terror and hatred. Too late, I realized she'd seen my freakish transformation, the glittering of my eyes, the expression of animalistic power on my face.

"I knew it!" she rasped. "I knew you were one of them...you're a beast!"

Chapter Twenty-Two
Lily

I took a deep breath and looked steadily at her. She scooted back against the tree, trying to get away from me.

"Avery…" I began, but she cut me off with a wild sort of scream.

"You *lied* to me! I knew it! I never should have trusted you!"

Her eyes bulged hysterically, making her look insane. I backed up a little, my head exploding with anger, fear, desperation and a little sadness. Avery and I had become allies, friends, and at the first sign of trouble she lost it.

"Can I please just explain?" I asked.

"Why should I let you? How can I trust you?"

I took a few steps toward her, making her cower. "Listen, I wasn't completely honest, I'll admit." I crossed my arms, suddenly uncomfortable. No one but Wes and mom knew what I really was, and I'd preferred to keep it that way. But…

"Avery, I'm…half beast." There. I said it.

She narrowed her eyes. "You expect me to believe that?"

"My dad, as you know, was an original beast. He was in the first group tested. He transformed more slowly than the others." A lump formed in my throat as the memory of his crude grave surfaced in my mind. I closed my eyes briefly for composure.

"He must have known what would eventually happen to him because he couldn't just abandon my mom. He went to see her one last time and I…was the result."

The hardness in Avery's face softened only slightly as she cocked her head. "Why would your mom do that?"

"I told you. My dad didn't go as fast as some of the others. She said his eyes were a little off and he was pale, but other than that he looked normal."

The hatred etched into Avery's face slowly melted into disbelief, then curiosity. "So what did it do to you, then? I mean, if it's true."

I kicked at some pebbles nearby. "We don't really know. All we know is that I don't get sick often. When I do, I recover pretty quickly. I've always been a very good athlete."

"And the...the side effects?"

"They weren't really noticeable until a few months ago. My mom was really sick with cancer, and we couldn't afford the treatment. My emotions were completely out of whack. That's when the beast gene or whatever it is kicks in. But I can't do claws or anything like that. Just eyes and super-human strength."

Pity slowly crept into Avery's eyes. "Did she...did your mom..."

"No," I replied abruptly. "I told you, remember? I...found a way to get the cure, at a price."

"What do you mean?" She sat up now, her eyes fully bright with curiosity, with...greed. I sighed inwardly, knowing exactly what she was thinking.

"The Mainframe. I made a deal with Vic from defense. I offered to become part of his army, let his scientists study me, in exchange for full payment for my mom's treatment."

She took in a sharp breath. "That's why you ran."

I nodded. "My mom's safe up north, as far as I know, but I've gotta find her soon. I have no idea what they'll do to her if they locate her."

Avery blew out a breath and drew her knees up to her chest. She looked up at me, hesitant.

"I know what you want," I mumbled. "A cure. For Trent, for the beasts, for everybody."

She shrugged, a sheepish grin playing across her freckled face. "Well...the thought did cross my mind."

"Yeah, but how would we figure out a cure? I'm *not* going back to the Mainframe and turning myself in. You have no idea what they're capable of."

She sat up a little and smiled mischievously. "Why would I send you back to the Mainframe? I'm not that cruel. Besides, you forget that we have a whole group of trained scientists in our vicinity, bent on bringing down the Mainframe."

I gave a short laugh of contempt. "Yeah, beasts that'll kill us on contact. Don't think it's gonna happen."

"But what about Trent? If we could somehow find him, talk with him, he could convince the beasts to join us. I'm sure they'd jump at the chance for a cure."

I frowned skeptically, my hands on my hips. "How would we get to Trent?"

"Same way they got him off the island. Simple."

"Kidnap him?" I laughed again. "You've got to be kidding."

"Hey, what have we got to lose? We're both outlaws, pretty much. If we don't do anything, nothing will ever be fixed."

I walked a few slow circles, thinking hard. "Yeah, good point, but how are we going to get back over the border? Especially with your ankle out of commission?"

Before I could stop her, she struggled to her feet. She took a few jerky steps, wincing in pain.

"Well...I think it's just a bad sprain. If we rest here for the night, I should be able to make it. I'm a tough old bird."

I just shrugged. Avery and I had only known each other a short time, but I knew better than to argue with her. After I hunted down some more berries and nuts for the journey across the border, we settled down to try and sleep the rest of the night. Avery soon dropped off, but I stared up at the stars for a long time before I finally faded.

A warm ray of sun across my face woke me a few hours later. Avery was already up, stepping gingerly around the clearing on her newly bandaged leg. She'd torn some cloth from her pants to wrap the ankle more firmly. Both of us pretty much now wore shorts and t-shirts, having torn off so much cloth for bandaging.

"Gather some more food, this won't be near enough," she commanded in her usual leader-like tone. I gathered the meager provisions into my shirt and gripped it with one hand to keep them from spilling. With the other arm, I supported Avery.

Angling ourselves away from the morning sun, we headed north back up into the mountains. The going was rough and slow since Avery had to take several breaks, but she insisted on keeping on. With no visible trail to follow, we stumbled several times, Avery biting her tongue to keep from crying out in pain. Near noon, we ran into a steep incline that rose about six feet before leveling out. I stopped and stared at it, still supporting Avery.

"So...what do we do now?"

I looked at her and she shrugged. "It's good practice for the border fence."

I felt my eyes pop out in surprise. "The border fence? You mean we're going to try and hop it?"

"How else are we going to get back?"

I slapped my hand to my forehead. "Avery, I'm pretty sure it's topped with barbed wire!"

"Not every part of it. They don't keep it in very good repair. Part of it could have fallen off."

"This is insane," I replied. "It's never going to work."

"Look, you have super human strength, right? All you have to do is get to the top and pull me up."

"Avery..."

"Let's just get over this thing and we'll worry about the fence when we come to it."

"Fine," I muttered. I walked up to the wall of dirt before me and suddenly felt scared. The height of it made my heart began to pound. I'd seen waves much bigger than this thing, and yet it just felt insurmountable.

I swallowed hard, headed back to where Avery stood, and faced the incline. With a deep breath, I crouched as if readying for a race, then took off. The wall came up fast. I jumped as hard as I could, scrambled for the top and smacked face first into the dirt.

As I clutched my bleeding nose, I looked back at Avery with contempt. "See?"

"You've got to wait until you get up to it. You jumped too soon."

"I suppose you could do better?" I shouted. Blood pumped furiously through my veins, making my heart thrum in my chest.

"You can do this, Lily. Stop being such a baby."

I lunged at her, my mind gone, a strange heat behind my eyes. She stared at me calmly and smiled. "Direct it at the incline."

"What?"

"Just do it! Head for the wall again!"

Too angry to argue, I turned and rushed for the wall. The tiny part of me that remained sane felt the same fear, but my legs were pumping madly towards the dirt ahead of me. I took a foot up onto the dirt, propelled myself up to the flat, grabbed some random tufts of grass and hoisted myself up.

When I stood up and looked back, my anger slowly melted and turned into disbelief. Avery stood below, smiling benignly.

"You got me mad on purpose."

"Partly," she replied.

I turned around, cursing under my breath. I knew Avery did what she had to do, but part of me still felt angry. Already she was using me for my abilities, just as the Mainframe would have done. I thought about leaving her behind. It would be far easier to just go and hurry across the border my own way, but a surge of guilt suddenly overwhelmed me as I remembered how she rescued me in the Shadowlands.

Still irritated, I reluctantly reached down and helped her climb up. She tore yet another swatch of cloth and directed me to press it to my nose until the bleeding stopped. We ate a quick lunch, drank from a nearby stream, and continued up the mountain. My stomach rumbled harshly for what must have been the thousandth time. I felt so hungry and tired that all I wanted to do was collapse on the dirt and never move again. Avery's ankle also started to swell again, turning red and puffy. She needed rest badly, but she refused to stop under any circumstances.

At long last, as the sun began to dip in the sky, the menacing border fence came into view. Directly ahead of us, the tall metal loomed with looped barbed wire over it, charged and ready to electrocute. Fear gripped me.

"See? I told you," I hissed.

"Fine, we'll just go down along the fence that way until we hit a part with no wire."

I gazed to my left. The wire stretched on for miles, as far as I could see. To the right, the wire stretched out a good length before being interrupted by a guard station.

"Which way?" I hissed. "There's more wire one way and a guard the other."

Avery bit her lip, staring in each direction for a long time. "Maybe we can get through when the guard falls asleep."

I rolled my eyes. "Avery, this isn't 2050. I'm sure they have a night guard ready to take the day guard's place."

"Then you think of something!" she snapped. "I'm tired of you always looking at me to be the hero, to figure a way out of messes. For once, *you* do something!"

"Hey, you're the one taking advantage of me for this curse that I've got. You and Vic would be real good pals!"

"How *dare* you compare me to that…that psycho?" she practically screamed. "He took my husband away, and now you're saying I'm like him?"

"You provoked me into getting mad just so-"

I stopped, choking on my words. A small but burly man suddenly emerged from the guard station, looking around for the source of the noise.

"Hide!"

Chapter Twenty-Three
Lily

I grabbed Avery's arm and yanked her into a clump of bushes. The sharp little prickles jabbed harshly into my skin, making me bite my tongue to keep from yelling out.

"Don't move," I whispered to her. We still had a clear view of the guard, wandering around and peering intently through the trees. He shaded his eyes against the late summer sun and walked a little farther into the trees, convinced he'd find something. We were lucky to be a little to the west of him. He thought the noise was straight ahead.

As I watched him, a brilliant idea slowly dawned on me. I traced his movements carefully, noting how he retreated deeper into the woods, then seemed to think better of it. Finally, he seemed to give up and headed back to the tower with a few suspicious glances behind his back.

"Avery...we can get through the border there! In the tower!"

She rolled her eyes at me. "Yeah...how exactly are we going to do that?"

I motioned towards the thick clump of trees across from the tower. "Didn't you see how he poked around back there? He doesn't seem like the type to give up easily. What if we drew him out enough to keep him busy while we slip through the tower?"

"I'm sure he's not the only one, remember?" she replied with a sarcastic look.

"Well, do you have any better plan?" I shot back, using her own ammo against her as she'd done to me. "Besides, if we draw one out enough, maybe the other will come investigate too."

She crossed her arms. "How are you going to draw them out?"

"Watch," I offered. I stepped cautiously from the bushes after double checking that the guard had definitely gone back to his post. A large, egg shaped rock lay on the ground beside me. I picked it up and swiftly hurled it into the woods across from the tower, then ducked into the bushes again. The same guard came running out, a look of irritation on his square face. He looked around slowly, then ventured into the woods again. As soon as his back turned, I stepped from the bushes again and hurled another rock, farther into the woods this time.

"What the-" The pudgy man scratched his head.

I listened to the guard muttering to himself as I stifled my giggles. Avery peered through the foliage, watching him in disbelief.

"Isn't he trained to stay near the tower? How dumb can he be?" she muttered. I ignored her, too thrilled that my plan was working. I threw one last rock, then chanced a glance at the tower. No one came out, and the guard didn't call out to anyone. I was sure he would've by now.

"It's now or never. We've gotta go while he's distracted," I said. "Let's go."

Avery grabbed my arm. "Hang on, nobody followed him out. What if there's another guy in there?"

"I think we've waited long enough. He would have called for help by now."

For good measure, I threw another rock, farther out in a different direction to confuse him. I heard the satisfying rustle of his bulky body pushing through the brush, hunting for a quarry he'd never find.

"Come on!" I hissed. Reluctantly, Avery followed me out. We darted as quickly as we could, staying hidden as well as possible.

We reached the open door and peeked inside. A long hallway, with another branching off to the right, stretched before us. A door stood straight across from the other one, making a sort of T-shaped structure with the door to one side facing the door to the other side. I stifled a shout of glee. We were as good as home.

I waltzed in confidently, knowing the guard would continue to search through the woods for a while. Suddenly, Avery yanked me by the arm back towards the door we'd just come through. I started to protest until she firmly clapped a hand over my mouth and pointed down the other hall. A guard sat there, looking bored. For a moment, I caught my breath. He looked strangely…familiar, but his face was angled away from me as he peered out the window at the other guard. She took her hand away from my face and mouthed "Told you."

I rolled my eyes angrily and shrugged. So there was another guard. It wasn't like we couldn't sneak past. He wasn't watching the hallway, after all.

I took Avery's arm and tiptoed quietly across the opening towards the other door. We made it without the guard noticing anything. I pushed open the door quietly, but to my horror, an alarm began to blare loudly. The door had been rigged!

I looked at Avery, frozen. She stared back, both of us feeling suddenly very exposed. I considered shutting the door to keep the alarm quiet, but I heard the rustle and squeak of a chair. The guard was coming. I wrenched the door open and bolted without a second thought.

I looked behind me and saw Avery running and stumbling away from a guard who stood at the door. Even through my panic, I realized he seemed so familiar, but I couldn't place it. He was too far away to recognize him for sure. I slowed a little, waiting for Avery to catch up.

Finally, she came within ten feet of me. We put on an extra burst of speed and shot through the trees and dense foliage. I looked back again and noted with relief that we'd lost the guard, but they'd catch up before long.

"A tree!" I shouted, completely out of breath. "We need…a tree!"

"What?" Avery hollered back.

I couldn't talk, so I just pointed at a promising tree ahead with several low limbs. I jumped onto it and scaled it quickly, pausing to help Avery up where I could. We climbed higher and higher until it became impossible to climb anymore. As we clung to smaller branches near the top, we paused to catch our breath. Soon, two sets of voices came into the clearing. I motioned her to quiet her breathing.

"They can't have gotten far!" one shouted.

"They could have gone anywhere, Krantz," the other muttered. Something about that voice jarred me. I knew it, but how? Where had I heard it before? The familiarity was driving me crazy. For a moment, I thought of Wes, but it was impossible. Why would he be on border patrol for Epirus?

"Start looking! They could have gone up a tree, or holed up somewhere in some cave."

"Look, let's just go back. These woods give me the creeps, anyway."

"Oh, give me a break, you don't really believe all that garbage about beasts, do you? You Illyrians have always been so superstitious."

Illyrians?! My heart sped up, hopeful. Was it him? But then, he had to have recognized me. Why would he run after me like that?

"I just don't wanna be here. So what, a few girls got across. It's not like they'll live long out here."

A sharp pain stabbed at my heart. If it was Wes, how could he say those things? Why would he? Without warning, hot tears sprang to my eyes and splashed down my face.

The other man, Krantz, let out a long sigh. "Fine. It's almost quitting time for me, anyway."

I inched around the tree and peeked down. I could barely see the men standing there. I wondered for a moment if they were waiting to see if we appeared. Finally, they started to wander off back towards the tower. I watched them until they disappeared from the trees, then let out the breath I'd been holding. I forced myself to regain composure, then looked at Avery.

"That was a close one," I murmured. She glared at me.

"Yeah, you think? Maybe try listening next time before you just make a break for it."

"Hey, we got away, didn't we?" I shot back.

I started to climb down, but Avery stopped me. "The sun's almost down," she cautioned. "I don't know if the beasts go this far south, but it's probably not a good time to come down. The ones that are far gone are more active at night."

I shrugged, a little annoyed I hadn't thought of that, but let it go. She was right, and I certainly wasn't willing to repeat my experience with another far-gone beast bent on killing me.

"How are we going to sleep up here?" I asked.

She glanced around. "There's a thicker branch down there. Why don't we sit on that and take it in shifts? One of us can keep an eye on the other and make sure they don't fall out, the other can sleep."

I readily agreed, suddenly realizing how tired I felt. Guilt crept into my consciousness, however, when I noticed Avery gingerly touching her ankle. I'd completely forgotten about her injury. Adrenaline must have pushed her to run, but she paid for it now. I tore some more cloth from my pants and helped her wrap her ankle tightly. Her eyelids drooped heavily, so I offered to take the first shift. She looked up into the darkening sky.

"If I remember right, it's a quarter moon tonight. Wake me up when the moon is there," she instructed, pointing off into the east."

I nodded and she settled down in a large knot where the branch met the trunk. As the darkness grew, I worried about keeping myself awake, not to mention keeping Avery in the tree, but the cold soon took care of that.

It suddenly struck me that fall had come. The air felt so much colder at night, even down on the flat out of the mountains. I had no idea what day or month we were even in anymore, but it had to be at least late August or possibly even September. Though the trees were mostly pine in this neck of the woods, a few had started to change their leaves.

I crouched over a few times to stabilize Avery, all the while keeping an eye on the moon. The moon reached the indicated point after an hour or so, but Avery slept so soundly that I felt terrible waking her. I rubbed my arms, trying to keep warm, and looked down at the forest floor for something to do. I hadn't really expected to see anything, so I had to bite down hard on my cheeks to keep from screaming. A shadowy figure lurked below, wandering around and looking for something. I could tell by the way he hunched, his claws flexing, that he was a beast. A far-gone one by the look of it.

I swallowed hard and leaned back, trying to steady my breathing and my racing heart. I made sure Avery sat steadily in the tree, then looked down again. The thing prowled around a while longer, then wandered off to the east until I couldn't see him anymore. Though he'd gone, my heart still pounded until the sky finally began to turn gray and pink with approaching dawn.

I leaned back against the branch, my eyelids feeling like someone filled them with cement. Avery still slept, crouched comfortably in the little knot in the tree. I wanted sleep so badly, but still couldn't bring myself to wake her. She had an injury. She needed to sleep. I needed sleep...

Somehow, I found myself back on Lander's beach, our beach. As promised, Wes stood there, his curly hair mussed as if he'd just gotten up, his boyish face beaming at the sight of me.

"Where have you been?" he asked with a little laugh. "I was starting to think someone got you."

I wanted to laugh, but the remark seemed a little off somehow. I started to ask him what he meant, but a growl suddenly sounded behind me. I turned and my heart stopped as I recognized Jensen from the island.

"What are you-"

I stopped talking as he lunged. I ducked and suddenly a strange feeling of weightlessness overtook me.

My eyes snapped open just as I slid off the branch. Giving a little scream, I reached out, scrambling with my arms, but to no avail. Suddenly, a pair of cold hands gripped mine with iron strength. I looked up to see Avery's face above mine.

"What happened? Why didn't you wake me up?" she shouted, her face red with anger and fear.

I started to explain when suddenly her face went ash white.

"Don't move," she mouthed.

I looked down below me and felt my insides freeze. A dozen or so beasts stood at the base of the tree, staring up at us with hatred etched in their blazing red eyes.

Chapter Twenty-Four
Wes

The next few days passed in a blur that Wes barely registered. He went through training for the border patrol post amidst constant bombing and attacks. Conley became a close friend, persuading others to see beyond Wes's nationality and accept him as an ally in the war.

Wes felt secure here, but he ached every second for Lily. His sleep was continually plagued with nightmares of her caught by Vic, caught by southern soldiers, of never seeing her again. He knew he could easily stay here forever, in safety, but how would he ever find her? It would be a half-life, nothing worth living without her.

The morning finally came in which he'd take up his post, but he put on his uniform half-heartedly. He'd tried everything he could think of to assuage his fears, but nothing helped. He tried to imagine where he'd go if he were Lily and found some solace in the fact that she was so smart, so capable of taking care of herself and others, but so many forces were working against her it was impossible for him not to worry. And who was this mysterious person she traveled with? How had they met up? Could this person be trusted?

All these thoughts swirled around in his mind on the drive to the border, making him feel a little ill.

"You still worried about your girl?" Conley asked conversationally.

Wes shrugged. "How can I not be?"

"I'm sure she made it. Maybe she was as lucky as you and found a friend like me." He grinned, that self-assured humor coming out again. Through all the rage of the war, Conley somehow managed to stay cheerful and optimistic.

"Maybe," Wes replied, though he didn't feel too sure anymore.

As they pulled to a stop in front of a small office, he climbed out quickly, eager for some distraction. The office sat seemingly in the middle of nowhere, attached to a large fence topped with barbed wire.

A small man with a huge mustache bustled out of the office and approached the car. He gave a friendly nod when he saw Conley, but looked at Wes warily.

"This the guy?" he grunted unceremoniously.

Conley nodded. "Krantz, this is Wes Landon. Wes, this is Ed Krantz. He's been at this post for years, and his partner was called into the Rescue Team. That's why we needed a replacement."

Krantz walked over and stood in front of Wes, his face pulled in an ugly frown. Wes knew right away they were not going to get along, but he offered his hand. Krantz shook it, his expression remaining the same.

"So you're a Baby, eh?" Wes fought the impulse to punch him. The term was slang, implying Illyrians couldn't get their own food and had to be fed like babies. He couldn't resist shooting the nasty name for Epirians back at him.

"Yep. So that makes you a Superian." It was harsh, but this guy was looking for a fight and Wes wasn't about to cower with his tail between his legs. Epirus had long been known for its superiority complex, but had always suffered humiliating defeat by several other countries years back. It had only recently gained independence to then be invaded by Illyria.

Krantz narrowed his eyes threateningly at the jeer as Conley smiled nervously. "Hey now, guys, we're all on the same side. Even Landon here admits he's an ex-pat."

"Just take orders and keep quiet," Krantz snapped.

Wes looked at Conley with an expression that clearly said "Get me out of here," but he either acted or was completely oblivious.

"I'll come check on you in a week or so. Good luck."

With a quick clap on the back, he headed back to the car. Wes gathered his extra uniform and underclothes and followed Krantz into the office. The small room on the first floor included a room with weapons, phones and two large windows that looked out either side of the border. Two doors stood on opposite ends as well, each equipped with a secure bar.

"Kitchen's back of this room," said Krantz, gesturing vaguely. "Upstairs is two rooms, yours is on the left. Your first night on duty is tonight, then we'll switch."

He walked into the windowed room and gestured at the phones. "This one calls patrol station five. This one calls patrol station seven. We're six. If there's an invasion, we call both of them and they carry on the signal to other offices on the border. Got it?"

"Who does this one call?" Wes asked, pointing to a prominent red set with a large screen.

"The police. Any more questions?" Wes shook his head. "Good. Get some sleep then."

Wes walked slowly up the stairs, a little annoyed that Krantz had purposely put him on second shift. He'd just slept the whole night through and wouldn't be able to sleep at all.

Wes wandered through the small room and attached bathroom, trying to figure out something to do. He didn't even have a book or any kind of personal possession. He put away his clothes in the compact dresser and laid down on the cot.

Sleep wouldn't come, so he got up and wandered around the room again, occasionally looking out the small, bulletproof window. On the fifth time around, he paused at the window and looked out again. Was it just his imagination, or had he seen a flash of white among the trees on the Epirus side?

He leaned closer to the window, squinting for a better view. Surely it was just his imagination, yet something inside him told him it wasn't. He saw it again-a distinct flash of white, like someone in a white shirt running through the trees. He hurried down the stairs and into the small windowed room.

"What are you doing down here?" Krantz barked. "I told you to go to sleep."

"I think I saw something," Wes replied. "Out in the woods. I think someone's walking around."

Krantz rolled his eyes. "Trying to get some excitement your first day? Give it up, Landon. All the action is at the docks. That's where the ground forces invade. No one would be fool enough to try and cross the border."

"I'm serious!" he shot back. "There's someone out there. Aren't you at least going to check?"

They were cut off abruptly by a shout. It sounded like an angry woman. Wes looked at Krantz smugly, whose face reddened.

"Fine," he blustered. "I'll so some checking. But you stay here."

He walked out and circled a few times, then came back. "Nothing there. Probably just a loose cougar or something."

Wes stared at him, irritated. A cougar didn't wear bright white clothes. He knew he'd seen something, but he wondered how he would ever convince this guy. The man obviously wouldn't believe anything unless he'd thought of it himself.

Krantz looked at the stairs pointedly. Wes rolled his eyes and started towards the steps when suddenly Krantz ran out again. Wes rushed to the window and looked out. Krantz ventured into the woods, looking as if he were listening intently.

"Oh now you look," Wes muttered. He sat down in his swiveling chair and leaned back, watching as Krantz wandered blindly into the woods, striding one way, then suddenly circling back and walking a different way. Whatever it was had him guessing. Wes stifled a laugh watching him waddle through the trees, looking completely confused and frustrated.

An alarm suddenly started to wail behind Wes, making him sit bolt upright. He ran to the hallway with the doors to find a woman standing there, pale and terrified. Her blondish hair stuck out in all directions, and she was covered head to toe in scratches and bruises. Her white shirt and pants were ripped and blood-stained. The two stared at each other for a split second before she suddenly took off, favoring her right leg slightly. Wes followed and noticed another girl with her, one with wavy brown hair that fell past her shoulders. She turned, looking for her companion, and I caught a brief glimpse of her face. *Lily!*

Without waiting to notify Krantz, Wes bolted into the forest after her.

Chapter Twenty-Five
Lily

I hung there helplessly as Avery stared at them, my arms aching and sweat beading my forehead and neck.

"Do you know who that is?" said a harsh voice.

"The girl," replied another raspy snarl. He gave a low chuckle. "What a stroke of luck for us!"

My whole body began to tremble, making my situation even more precarious. "Pull me up!" I whispered urgently. Avery sat on her perch, transfixed, seeming not to hear me.

"Avery!"

She looked down at me, finally realizing what I asked but seeming dazed. With a monumental heave, she pulled me up and helped me climb back onto the branch.

"They're after me," I hissed urgently. "We've got to get away!"

"Trent…" She gazed down at the group, her face a mix of elation and anguish.

"Avery!" Frustration rose in a crescendo inside me, making me feel almost sick. She couldn't think about anything else but her precious Trent.

"You girl! Come down here. We won't harm you," one of the beasts shouted up at us. I swallowed hard, trying to figure a way out of my predicament.

"Why?" I shouted back lamely.

"You know why. We know who you are." The group laughed sinisterly, making my blood freeze in its tracks.

"Then why would I want to come down? I'm pretty sure you're lying about not hurting me." I gripped the rough bark of the tree, knowing my time was short. If they wanted, they could hurl themselves up the tree after me.

"We just want to talk," came a very deep, very gruff voice, one that sounded somehow more gentle than the others. "Please. Besides, my wife is in that tree with you and I'd like to see her."

"You always were such a paddy, Donovan."

Avery started to climb down, the sadness gone from her face, her eyes shining with joy at her husbands' recognition. I gripped her arm harder than I meant to, and she wrenched free with a blazing glare.

"Are you crazy?" I muttered through gritted teeth, trying hard not to be heard. I had no idea how sound would travel from a tree top to the forest floor.

"My husband is down there, the man I love who I haven't seen for over a year. I'm not passing up this chance to talk to him. It's why I came to this terrible place."

"It could be a trap, Avery. Are you willing to just waltz in there with a group of other psychotic *beasts*?"

She just shrugged and continued to climb down. Helpless, I clung to the branch and watched her go. A few feet above the ground, she swung down on a low limb and leapt neatly to the ground. Avery hesitantly approached a beast, presumably Trent. They didn't hug or even touch, but it probably seemed really awkward to them to do that given the situation.

"Come on, girl! Join your friend down here! We didn't hurt her."

The voices of the other beasts rose in assent, making my heart race. They'd probably been secretly ordered by Trent not to hurt Avery, but who knew what they'd do to me? A bunch of crazy, diseased scientists desperate for a cure? No thanks.

And yet, I was slowly starving to death and, more immediately, thirsty. I hadn't slept properly in who knew how long and I wanted so badly to have a fresh change of clothes and even a dip in the freezing cold stream. I couldn't last in this tree forever.

I scanned the lower limbs, wondering how to get out of this mess, when a low-lying branch on the north side of the tree caught my eye. The beasts had all gathered around the south side of the tree, staring up at me expectantly, some jeering or mocking in loud tones. My eyes followed the branch northward, where through the trees I could see a slightly worn trail. If I could get down to it, run and veer off the trail at some point, I might be able to make it back to the cave somehow.

"Ok, fine," I called, pretending to concede. "I'll come down."

The beasts laughed and congratulated themselves, heartily slapping each other on the backs. "I knew something good would happen today," said one eagerly.

Though they completely disgusted me, a small part of me began to feel pity again for the creatures. Were they really so desperate that they'd harm me? I shuddered at the thought.

I climbed carefully down around the massive trunk, picking my steps carefully. To the beasts, I appeared to be climbing right down into their midst, when really I calculated every inch, every step I'd need to gain the advantage.

My pulse pounded in my head as I reached the last limb. "Come on, girl. We'll help you down."

One beast reached out his clawed fingers, a leering grin on his eerily pale face. I took one last deep breath, then swung around to the low branch on the backside of the tree. Using Avery's little move from before, I jumped to the ground and took off like a shot.

Angry, rasping voices rose behind me, but I couldn't concentrate on anything they said. I powered all my thoughts into my legs, willing myself to run faster until the trees became a brown blur around me. As I approached a thick clump of trees, I veered off the path and ran through the brush. The going became difficult what with upraised tree roots and low branches in my path, but my monster gene came in handy once again. I pulled on my hybrid strength, using it to guide me through the chaotic forest.

After I'd put about four miles behind me, I slowed gradually and ducked into some undergrowth. As my breathing slowed, I realized I heard no sounds, no crashing brush, no angry voices nearby. They could have easily kept up. Why hadn't they come?

I laughed a little, wondering why I cared. I'd gotten away, after all. I took a deep, quiet breath and sat back to relax for a while.

My adrenaline drained away, leaving me completely exhausted. Though hunger and driving thirst raged through my body, I couldn't summon the energy to forage. I laid down right there in the dirt, shaded by the cool, thick leaves of the bush around me, and fell asleep.

When I awoke, dusky light filtered into my hiding place. Night had begun to fall, and still no one had found me. I sat up and stretched my stiff muscles, my head aching from burning thirst.

Slowly, I crawled out of the leaves and dragged myself to my feet. Driven only by the intense need for water, I began to wander aimlessly, trying to listen for the rush of water over my heavy breathing and thudding footsteps.

I stopped after about ten minutes of trudging, hoping against hope that I hadn't heard wrong. No, it was there, the distinct babble of a stream. I bent down and put my ear to the ground, using a trick I'd seen Avery use in the mountains to find water. I heard the rush of the stream directly to my right. I tramped over a hill and down into a small valley, where a steady flow of water ran through a long, narrow patch of grass.

Gratefully, I fell on my knees and began to slurp the cold, delicious water. I cupped my hands and dumped some of the water over my head and onto my clothes, doing my best to wash out the grime.

Feeling like a new person, I leaned back against the stump of a huge tree and rested for a while. A funny sort of peace stole over me as I sat there. I'd come back to the Shadowlands, but they didn't frighten me as they had before. After all I'd been through in the last few weeks, I supposed nothing could scare me much now, except being captured by the beasts.

Hunger eventually drove me to my feet again. If water lay nearby, surely I could find food here. I looked around and was rewarded eventually with a full blackberry bush, another edible fruit Avery had taught me about. Though the tart berries still tasted good, I couldn't help but be a little sick of them. Avery explained they wouldn't be in season much longer, that they would start to shrivel, and she was right.

I wanted real food so badly I could hardly stand it. Even the same old boring canned goods from the Ration Center sounded good now. I wondered vaguely what Gerald had done when I stopped coming to work. No doubt my face was plastered all over the city now as the number one wanted criminal, as it had been on the highway.

For some reason, this thought and everything I'd been through just struck me as hilarious. I laughed so hard I fell on all fours, clutching my stomach.

"I must be insane," I mumbled to myself. I rolled over on my back and stared at the twinkling stars through the trees. In my state of somewhat crazy contentment, I drifted off to sleep again.

Before long, a crunching noise woke me. As consciousness sank in again, I realized the sound was someone crashing through the trees. I immediately thought of the beasts and went into a panic.

As the noises came closer, I searched desperately for a hiding place, but I'd fallen asleep in a very open clearing. With no other option, I quickly shinned a tree and nestled on a thick branch, hoping and praying that whoever wandered this way didn't see me.

After several minutes, a tall man burst into the clearing. He wore some kind of dark uniform. Though I was sure I'd never seen him before, he seemed so familiar, almost like some kind of long-lost relative. Why did everyone seem so familiar to me?

He noticed the water and half-walked, half-crawled to it. After drinking deeply and washing his face, he sat on the ground, his knees pulled to his chest for warmth. I watched his every move, my heart racing. From what I could see in the faint light from the stars, he wasn't a beast. He didn't crouch and crawl and rasp like they did when the Akrium had completely taken over.

An hour or so crept by as I watched him, but he didn't do anything, just sat there staring into the stream.

I inched across the branch, trying to get a closer look at him, but he hunched over so much that it became nearly impossible to distinguish any features.

I moved up the limb again, squinting in the darkness, but to no avail. I reached up to push some low-hanging leaves out of the way when a splintering noise sounded behind me. I looked back and noticed, to my horror, the branch giving way. Before I had time to react, I plunged to the forest floor, my chest hitting the ground with a sickening smack.

"Ughhhh…."

I raised my head slightly, my breath gone as the ground tilted and swayed before my eyes. As soon as the whirling stopped, I took a quick stock of my body. Every part of me ached, but I felt pretty sure nothing had been broken in the fall.

A freezing, iron-like hand clamped suddenly around my arm and hauled me to my feet. For one wild moment, I thought the deranged beast from my first foray into the Shadowlands returned to finish me off, but I didn't see burning red eyes or frightening pallor, just a man's angry red face staring at me.

"Who are you?" he barked. "Where did you come from?"

"I...I..." I stuttered, trying to formulate some kind of excuse, but words simply failed me.

"Talk!" He looked slightly manic, his eyes bulging in his shadowed face. Then suddenly, he took in a sharp breath. His fingers reached out and touched my face, caressing my cheek. I smacked him away, feeling my beast-like strength rise in me once again.

"Get *off* me!" I grunted, summoning the power within me to push him off. "Why don't you talk? Who do you think you are, tramping through here acting all tough and then touching me like that?"

"Lily?"

Once again, I felt as if all the air had left my body. That voice, the voice I'd heard in my dreams, spoke here before me now. I shook my head, sure I was hallucinating. The beasts had probably put their poisonous herbs in the air here, too.

"How do you know my name? Who *are* you?"

He stepped slowly from the shadows into a small patch of light made by faint moonlight. Tears crept into my eyes at the sight of him. His curly hair had grown shaggy and unkempt, creeping down around his eyebrows. Those hazel eyes, the ones that captivated me so many times, sparkled in the light, but a dead sort of hollowness had come into them somehow. The boyish smile, so kind and confident, faltered slightly as he stared at me.

"Wes...how did you...where..."

A strange memory slowly crept into my consciousness as I stared at him, the time as a little girl when I'd been playing in the water at the beach. Without realizing it, I'd stepped into a rip tide and gradually gone farther out to sea. Mom had told me how to get out of a rip tide, but the water pounded over me so hard, making me feel completely overwhelmed and unable to swim. Someone on shore had to rescue me because I couldn't save myself. I felt now as I did that day, totally helpless as waves of fear and doubt and sorrow pounded over me.

"Lily, I can't believe..."

His words faded around me as I collapsed to my knees.

Chapter Twenty-Six
Wes

"What do you think you're doing?" Wes heard Krantz bellow from far away, but he didn't turn back. He couldn't. The longing inside him pushed him forward, making it nearly impossible to restrain himself. Yet he knew he couldn't follow her just yet…Krantz would get suspicious. He might even be moved from the border. The thought make him shiver a little.

Krantz caught up surprisingly quick for a pudgy guy and pulled Wes up short. "Trying to escape, eh? Was that whole charade a ruse to get rid of me so you could run off?"

"No, there are girls, they escaped," Wes panted. "Look!"

He pointed, thanking his lucky stars that the other girl hobbled slow enough for Krantz to get a glimpse of her and know he hadn't lied. When Krantz started towards her, though, Wes realized he needed a plan to keep Krantz away from them. Wes knew he'd promised to be an ally in the war, but Lily mattered far more than whose side he was on now. He decided he'd lure Krantz back to the post on the pretense of not catching the girls, then head back out into the forest when Krantz fell asleep that night. The thought of leaving Lily made him clench his fists in frustration, but it would be better this way. He had to keep Lily safe.

They ran for about ten minutes, then lost track of their quarries, making Wes secretly glad. He paused and leaned on his knees, pretending to catch his breath.

"What are you doing?" Krantz panted, slowing down. He paused near a large tree and took several deep breaths. "Come on!"

"We lost them, Krantz."

"They can't have gotten far!" he argued.

"They could have gone anywhere, Krantz," Wes replied, praying Krantz would give up. He was right, they couldn't have gotten far, especially the one with the injury, but Wes hoped his acting would hold up and convince the angry little man.

"Start looking! They could have gone up a tree, or holed up somewhere in some cave."

"Look, let's just go back," Wes said, trying to sound nonchalant. "These woods give me the creeps, anyway."

"Oh, give me a break, you don't really believe all that garbage about beasts, do you?" He laughed jeeringly. "You Illyrians have always been so superstitious."

Wes bit his tongue, trying not to lash out at him about just how real the beasts were. "I just don't wanna be here. So what, a few girls got across. It's not like they'll live long out here."

Krantz finally let out a long sigh. "Fine. It's almost quitting time for me, anyway."

Wes breathed a silent sigh of relief and followed Krantz back to the post. He tried to keep composure and not reveal his absolute elation over finding Lily alive, but it was difficult. The day passed slowly. Krantz took up his post and Wes laid on the small bed, feeling trapped and trying not to fidget. The only thing that kept him busy was thinking of Lily, knowing with keen satisfaction that he'd see her again soon, hold her in his arms, kiss her…

"Wake up, Landon. Your shift," said a gruff voice above him. He'd drifted off somehow, and woke to see Krantz standing above him. Krantz pointed to the stairs in his usual Draconian way, then headed to his small room. Wes went downstairs to the small patrol room and took a seat after eating an apple from the kitchen and sneaking a few in his pocket for Lily.

Before long, he heard loud snores coming from Krantz's room, but waited an extra half hour for good measure. The wait felt excruciatingly long, but he finally stood and crept towards the door. As he went to open it, however, he noticed an alarm system attached. He figured once he lifted the bar, a siren would most definitely sound. Krantz hadn't bothered to let him know the code to disarm the door. Then again, he'd probably done it purposely to keep Wes from leaving.

He stared at the door, lost. Krantz would be after him in a matter of minutes, along with the Epirian police. Then again…maybe they'd think it a waste of time.

Wes thought of Conley too, and felt a little twinge of guilt. He'd helped Wes so much, stood up for him when he thought no one would. He'd kept Wes from going to jail, or worse, being killed. And now, here he stood, ready to betray Conley.

But was it really a betrayal? Lily was more important to him than anything. He couldn't live out his life, comfortably sitting in an office while she lived life on the run. He knew he'd never forget the look of terror in her eyes, the look of someone who lived each moment fearing for her life.

Before he could hesitate anymore, he lifted the bar and pushed the door. As he'd predicted, a siren went off, but he bolted as hard and fast as he could towards the cover of the trees. Crashing through the brush, not really using a particular direction except away from the tower, he ran headlong. Wes had no idea if anyone chased him, but he plunged through the thick foliage, looking for a place to hide as quickly as possible.

At long last, he came to a thick clump of bushes and dove in, trying to ignore painful scratches from the thorns. He scrunched himself up small and waited, trying to catch his breath. Finally, his breathing slowed, but he heard no other sounds except the chatter of birds in the trees.

Eventually he drifted off, the fatigue from all the adrenaline finally overtaking him. When he woke, the sun had fully risen in the sky, its rays slanting through the leaves of the bush that surrounded him. He sat up slowly, feeling achy and sick. His legs felt tight, still burning from yesterday's furious run, but he stretched out and stood up to work out the stiffness.

After a quick check revealed no one nearby, he cautiously crept from his hiding spot. Wes realized Krantz and the others had probably given up, most likely using the time to secure the border better in case he came back.

It hit him suddenly how terribly thirsty he was. His throat felt raw from all the running the day before, and he hadn't had something to drink since before he'd gotten to the tower. He searched around for some water, pausing and listening every now and again for the sound of some kind of flowing stream.

After a while, he grew hungry too, but stubbornly held out on the apples since he'd intended to give them to Lily. Discouragement set in after a few hours as he realized he'd been a little too hasty, running after Lily when he didn't know for sure what would happen. Wes had little food and no water and was wandering around in some place he'd never been to.

Wes sat down for a break, trying again to listen for water, but to no avail. Fatigue overcame him again, and he slumped against a tree for some much needed sleep. He awoke a few hours later, groggy and feeling even more ill. The tight blue uniform he wore grated against his overheated skin, making him constantly itchy. The boots were new and a little too tight, making walking uncomfortable. He'd ditched his cap a long time ago, not caring anymore if anyone found it. The thick material was too hot on his head.

The sun finally lowered beyond the horizon and he stumbled around incoherently, wishing desperately that something would change. He needed water so badly that he could hardly walk. The evening air felt cool and pleasant on his fevered face, but his insides felt scorched.

As the stars began to pop out, he stopped suddenly and listened. Water. He knew he'd heard a stream nearby. He walked a few more steps and paused, but the water sounded farther away. He turned back and headed in the other direction. The stream suddenly loomed ahead, winding through a large clearing between a couple hills. He ran fast, crashing loudly through the brush. Anyone for miles around would hear him, he knew, but he was so thirsty he didn't care. He stumbled to the bank of the stream at last and fell on his knees, slurping up the water as fast as he could.

Satisfied, he sat back and hugged his knees to his chest. Fall had definitely come. The air grew cold enough to make him wish he had the heavy jacket from the recruits in the Mainframe. He sat there, his legs scrunched up until they fell asleep, thinking about Lily, hoping she was safe wherever she was.

A loud crash suddenly sounded behind Wes, making his heart start racing immediately. He jumped up and crouched, ready for an attack. A limp body lay nearby, the body of a girl. She groaned, and he noticed a broken tree limb next to her. Slowly, she got to her feet and stumbled slightly.

He flew to her side and yanked her up to her feet to face him. She could be a spy, she could be an insurgent or even…a beast.

"Who are you?" he yelled. "Where did you come from?"

"I…I…" she stuttered, but Wes shook her before she could say anything else.

"Talk!" Wes screamed in her face, feeling slightly barbaric. And then, as if he'd been hit with an electric bolt, he let her go and stepped back slightly. Her eyes caught the light of the moon, catching him by surprise. They were a delicate hazel-green color. He knew those eyes. He'd only seen eyes like that on one person. His heart leapt as his eyes wandered down the familiar curve of her cheek, around those beautiful lips to the brown curly hair that fell so thickly past her shoulders. He'd finally found her.

Chapter Twenty-Seven
Lily

My eyelids slowly fluttered open as I felt someone gently running a cool cloth over my head. Explosions of questions, doubts and memories ripped through my mind, making me feel ragged and weak.

Somehow I'd made it back to the cave, but how did Avery find me? Where had she even gone? Had everything just been some huge nightmare? As I strained through my muddled thoughts, I opened my eyes to a bizarre sight.

Wes sat above me, his hazel eyes staring down into mine, his hand lovingly caressing my burning face with some kind of cloth dipped in water.

"Wes? But…where's Avery?"

A look of confusion furrowed his brow. "Avery? Who's that?"

Slowly, the dots connected as my confusion melted away. I saw the fallen limb and remembered seeing him for the first time in months.

"A…a friend, I guess. I was traveling with her, but she…"

Then it dawned on me. I looked around fearfully, knowing the beasts had to be out looking. Night had fully fallen, the time when Avery said they were supposed to be out in full force. Or the long-gone ones, anyway.

"We've got to hide," I whispered tersely.

"What? Lily, what's going on?"

Without replying, I clutched his arm and stood up. Dizziness overtook me for a moment, but I managed to start trotting swiftly and silently through the woods, Wes at my heels. I looked around for a cave of some sort that we could hide in, especially since I didn't want to sleep in a tree again. Luck was with us as we rounded a large hill and found a tiny hole in the side.

"Wait here," I instructed, letting go of his hand. I crawled in and looked around as best I could in the dark. The cave was very small, but could easily fit us both. I took Wes's hand and we crept into the darkness.

His arms wound automatically around me, but I found myself pulling away, scared. Though I couldn't see his face, I knew he'd be hurt.

"I'm sorry, Wes," I faltered. "I…it's been a rough couple months and…"

I trailed off lamely. How could I tell him everything going through my head? How I'd been nearly killed so many times, how I'd been a prisoner of war, a refugee…I took a few deep breaths to steady myself. Slowly I eased into his arms, tried to get accustomed again to the feeling of being cared for. Yet as we sat there silently, I felt so aware of how much had changed since we'd last been together.

"Lily, we can't sit here like this forever. What's going on?" The sound of his voice brought back all the memories of the summer together, all our happy times on the beach, and suddenly I found myself sobbing into his shoulder as I'd done so many times before. He held me close as he'd always done, alternately stroking my hair and rubbing my back. Gradually my tears subsided, and I sat up so I could kind of face him in the dark.

"I'm sorry, I just…I still can't believe it. After all this hell, it's hard to believe that something good could happen."

"I know the feeling." Instead of his usual good-natured tone, his voice sounded dark, almost ominous. I shuddered a little, sensing more than just changes in his appearance.

"Wes, I…there's so much to tell you, but I don't know where to start."

"First of all, why did we have to hide?"

My cheeks burned. How could I have forgotten? He'd probably been sitting there the whole time wondering what was going on.

"The beasts, they…roam around this time of night. Or at least the far gone ones do."

"Far gone?"

"It means they're close to dying. The Akrium makes them grow abnormally large fingernail claw things, and turns their eyes red, and makes them lose their hair. Eventually, it kills them. So, they're all just here waiting to die."

"Whoa, whoa, whoa…hang on, you mean Akrium *kills* these guys?"

"Yeah."

"But does that mean-"

"I don't know," I cut him off, knowing from his tone what he was about to say. "But I don't think so. I'm only half-beast, and I don't seem to have any of the ill side effects."

"Oh." He clutched me tighter as if still afraid I might die. A small chuckle escaped my throat, more a laugh of relief than anything else. It felt so wonderful to be cared for again.

"Anyway, I ran here after...well, after everything."

"What happened that day on the beach? I thought you got away, I thought you'd be up north with your mom. This is the last place I ever expected to see you."

"No. It was all a trap. They got you, and knew I'd come after you. Vic found me and took me back to the Mainframe."

He drew in a sharp breath. "How did you get away?"

I laughed sarcastically. "You know how I can be. There was a big raid with a bunch of beasts everywhere, he got distracted but got me into the building. I woke up just as he and a team of freaks were going to come in and erase my memory. My beast glands or whatever they are worked major overtime and I managed to...um, beat him up."

Wes laughed, a laugh that filled the small cave and made me feel whole again. I'd forgotten how much I missed his easy laugh, his quick smile, his way of making me feel like things could never be wrong or horrible again.

"Wow! What a woman!"

I laughed too, the terror of the last few days seeming to fade away. "It sounds crazy now, but it scared the living daylights out of me when it was happening."

"So how'd you make it to the Shadowlands?"

"I ran for it. Cut through some back streets to the apartment, got some supplies and booked it for the beach. They almost got me there, and I got shot somewhere along the way, but I managed to get into the trees. It's a miracle, really, that they didn't catch up."

"You got *shot*? Where? Are you ok?"

"Relax," I replied. "Avery bandaged it up. It's fine now."

He gave a low whistle. "So...who is this Avery person you keep talking about?"

"I met her in the Shadowlands, she saved me from one of the beasts, one of the manic ones out of his mind."

"So what is she doing here?"

"Her husband..."

I trailed off, remembering Avery had gone with the beasts. I wondered vaguely for a moment what had happened to her, whether the beasts had turned on her. A small part of me felt guilt for running away as I had, but how could I trust them? How could I trust Avery for that matter, when she needed a cure just as badly as the rest of them? They might even be plotting to find me and experiment.

"Lily?"

I shook myself out of my thoughts. Avery would never do that...would she?

"Sorry, I just lost track of my thought. Um, her husband is a beast, one of the guys they did Akrium testing on. So she was looking for him, but we had a run in with them a while ago. She stayed with them and I ran."

"Why? Wouldn't you kind of have protection from her husband?"

"No...I...it's complicated. I don't trust them because they're hard pressed for a cure. I'm pretty sure they would do anything to get their hands on me."

He lapsed into silence, clutching me closer and closer all the time. I reached up and put my arms around his neck, letting my head fall on his shoulder.

"Wes?"

"Yeah?"

"What happened to you? I...I thought for a minute you became some kind of guard in Epirus because..."

I trailed off, noticing that he'd stiffened. "Yeah, I...I was. I...it's hard to explain. I knew it was you running away, and I made a plan to catch up."

"But...why would you tell that other guy that we'd die anyway?" Tears formed in my eyes again, but I forced them down.

"I was trying to get him away from you. I knew if he found you, they'd take you into custody. I came later and looked for you here for a couple days."

"But what happened before that? How'd you end up playing guard for the other side?"

Wes took a deep breath. "I don't think I can talk about it just now," he replied. I scooted away, a little angry.

"I told you what I've gone through. What's the deal with you?"

"I just don't want to talk about it!"

The finality in his voice was the final straw.

"Fine. Don't talk to me, but don't get mad if I don't talk to you," I snapped. I purposely faced away from him and laid down. He placed an arm gently on mine.

"I will tell you, I just really don't want to talk about it now," he offered quietly. "Please try to understand."

I longed to keep nursing my anger, but turned towards him instead.

"Well, I've been through a lot too, you know," I shot back.

"And I'm sure you haven't told me absolutely everything." A hint of humor rose in his voice. I gave him a playful shove.

"Ok, fine. Let's get some sleep, I'm bushed."

He wrapped his arms around me and cradled my head into the crook of his arm. "Sounds good," he whispered, sending chills up my spine.

Slowly, we drifted off to sleep in each other's arms, warm and comfortable in our little cave. For the first time in a long time, no awful nightmares plagued my sleep.

Warm light slowly crept into the cave, waking us both. I smiled up at him, glad to see his face clearly for the first time since we'd found each other. He had a few scrapes and bruises, but he otherwise looked the same. The only thing that had truly changed was the look in his eyes. They'd always looked full of hope and possibility, but all that had become shadowed somehow in the past months, like expensive silverware gone dull and flat.

He leaned down suddenly and brushed my lips with his. The electrifying feeling I'd forgotten ripped through me again, waking all my senses, yet making me dizzy at the same time. I hadn't realized how intensely I'd missed his touch, his kiss, the longing in his eyes. I reached up and pulled him towards me, letting his lips intoxicate me and his touch to evaporate all the terror I'd been loaded down with since he we'd been separated.

At last we broke apart, our arms still wound tightly around each other. He leaned his forehead against mine, breathing shallowly as some of the fire returned and filled the deadness in his eyes.

"I can't tell you how much I've missed you," he whispered.

"I missed you too," I replied, stroking his cheek.

We held each other a while longer, neither of us wanting to face the day or the tasks ahead of us, but the call of hunger and thirst refused to be ignored any longer.

I tried not to worry as I took his hand. "Are you hungry?"

"Starved. I could use a good cheeseburger right about now, loaded down with everything."

I wrinkled my nose in disgust, but my heart leapt funnily in my chest as I remembered talking about burgers the first time we really met. That day on the beach had only been three or so months ago, but now seemed like a different lifetime.

"I could use a good *plain* burger right now," I laughed. We crawled out, stretched and started walking.

"If we can find Avery's cave, she's got canned goods," I explained. "But she taught me where we could find some edible berries."

We tromped through the woods, alert for any sign of the beasts and for berry bushes. Finally I found a blackberry bush loaded down, and we gorged ourselves.

"What are these things?" Wes said after gulping down a huge handful.

"Avery called them blackberries. They're good, aren't they?"

He just nodded and ate some more. Soon after, we found a stream and drank until we couldn't hold anymore.

Though we were stuck in a mutation-freak filled forest, I felt elated for the first time in a long time. Wes and I finally talked about all we'd been through since we'd seen each other, though I noticed he kept his comments pretty general and vague. He was holding something back, but what?

"Wait a minute!" I stopped in my tracks as we walked through a shady grove of trees later in the day. "A stream ran past the cave. We should just follow it north and it should take us back there eventually."

Wes shrugged and took my hand, letting me lead the way. We found our way back to the little brook and followed it for what seemed like hours. Just as the sun began to dip below the horizon, I spotted a large hill that looked promising. I ran ahead a ways to circle it and cried out ecstatically when I realized it was Avery's cave.

"We're here!" I called in delight.

"Good, I'm starved," he replied with a grin. We went around the back to the entrance by the stream and wiggled into the small opening.

"Well, it's about time you got back," said a voice in the main room. As my eyes adjusted to the evening dimness, I stepped back against Wes and grasped his hand. "We've been waiting all day."

Avery stood there next to a tall beast, her eyes trained steadily on me, a look of determination and exultation in her eyes.

Chapter Twenty-Eight
Lily

"Avery?" I stared at her, stunned. Why had she come back here? Why didn't she go with the beasts to wherever they lived?

"Lily." It wasn't a question, or really a statement. She just...said it. I grabbed Wes's hand, terrified.

"Avery, I'm not going with you and I'm not going along with whatever scheme these maniacs have cooked up," I muttered. "I came here for refuge. You got what you wanted, so just please leave me alone."

She smiled, a smile neither friendly nor malicious. It seemed a little strained. "You honestly don't trust me, do you? You never have."

I stared at her, unsure what to say. Of course I didn't trust her, but I didn't think I'd always distrusted her. We'd become friends, or really allies, but I trusted her before. Or had I? After all, I'd kept my secret for as long as I could.

"I did trust you once, but I think your determination to find a cure is overwhelming everything else," I replied evenly. "And I'm sorry, but I will not be used for a cure. I've already been hounded enough by the Mainframe."

She held up her hands. "All right, all right, yes, we do want a cure." She looked long and hard at Wes. "I take it this is the boyfriend?"

I looked at him hesitatingly. She could use him as leverage against me. I had to say something, but how could I keep his identity secret?

"Yes, I am, and you're not touching her," he shot back. I cringed inwardly. Though his heartfelt attempt to protect me was flattering, he'd just ruined any chance I had to protect him.

"Look, Avery, just tell me what you want," I cut in before she could reply.

"Trent and the others have extensive knowledge of DNA and mutations. It's how they figured out what would eventually happen to them, only they didn't realize it until after the actual injections. They thought the Akrium would only enhance strength and longevity, but the other side effects weren't anticipated. So if they could just test your DNA and see what is different, they might be able to figure something out."

"What exactly does that involve? The people at the Mainframe said I would have to have my memory wiped, and I figured I'd probably eventually be killed."

Trent laughed suddenly, scaring all of us, even Avery. The sound was nowhere near funny or charming, but a harsh, rasping cough sound. He stared at me intently with an unsettling look in his eyes.

"Those idiots don't know what they're doing," he rasped. "They lost all their best scientists and used poor, unsuspecting citizens to test. Of course they wouldn't know how to do a simple DNA test."

I tried to keep my cool as I gazed at Trent, but his very appearance brought back memories of my first day in the Shadowlands with the beast who'd tried to kill me. His eyes weren't completely red and he didn't have quite the look of a far-gone beast, but he was close.

"Look," he rasped, "all we would have to do is get a sample of hair, saliva, skin, anything that will show your DNA patterns. Then we'd compare it to ours. Simple as that."

"Yeah, and I suppose you'd just let me go free after that," I muttered.

"We're asking you to join us," he replied evenly. "Your father was a fine man. Avery told me what happened to him. You want to just let that go? Or do you want to revenge him for all that the Mainframe inflicted on him and your family?"

"Sympathy tactics? You've got to be kidding me." I folded my arms and started flatly at him. "You know this is about your revenge, not mine. Don't even bluff like that to me, you have no idea what my life has been like."

"I knew your father very well, and he was a good man. Since he was good, I know you're good too. I was on the island with him until the morons I live with kidnapped me and took me back here so we could raid the Mainframe for weapons and supplies. It's not just my revenge I'm looking for. I want revenge for every good man and their families that have been affected by this."

"Didn't you go to the island in the first place because you didn't want revenge?"

"Yes," he rasped harshly. "But I realized eventually what I was doing to my family. I don't agree with everything the beasts do, but if I could find a cure and bring them home, it would be worth any sacrifice."

"Including me," I challenged.

"As I told you before, people at the Mainframe don't know what they're talking about. We don't intend to harm you. We just need help."

I closed my eyes for a second, trying to sort through all the masses of thoughts and emotions swirling through me. I couldn't do what they asked…could I?

I looked at Wes, who seemed thoroughly confused. He looked at me questioningly, and I motioned him aside.

"Can we just talk for a minute?"

Trent shrugged and turned away, raking a hand through his thinning hair.

"What do you reckon?" Wes asked nervously.

"I don't know. I can't tell if he's lying or not," I replied, chancing a glance over my shoulder at him. What I saw startled me. Avery leaned against the cave wall, her arms folded, lips pursed, her eyes fixed on the floor. Trent stood a ways behind her, a horrible expression on his face, the look of a tortured man. I'd never seen such pain-filled eyes, such a haggard face. In that instant, my heart broke for him, for all the men affected by the injections. I thought again of my father's makeshift grave on an unknown island, no proper burial or goodbye. I'd never even known him.

I turned back to Wes, a feeling of heaviness weighing on my shoulders. "I…guess it can't hurt to do a simple test."

Wes gently grabbed my arm and tilted my chin up so he could look into my eyes. "Are you sure about this?"

I shrugged. "We probably don't have much choice, anyway. We could run, but it's either back to the city or back south to Epirus."

Wes's face darkened at the mention of the latter. "Well, at least we'll be together now. I won't let them do anything crazy."

I took his hand and turned to face the couple. Their behavior suddenly struck me as odd. They stayed far apart, barely looked at each other and seemed uncomfortable instead of joyful. Seeing Wes again, albeit under strange circumstances, had been like a breath of fresh air after feeling stifled so long. Things felt strange at first, mostly because of the amount of time we'd been separated, but it quickly melted away into our old feelings for each other. Avery and Trent seemed almost scared at the sight of each other.

"All right," I said, "I'll agree to one DNA test. But I'm not promising anything else until the scientists analyze the DNA and present a next step."

Trent's marred face broke into a smile for the first time ever since I'd met him. It wasn't really reassuring or even nice to look at, considering the disgusting state of his teeth, but I knew it was a genuine smile of gratitude.

"If it's all right, we'll camp here and go to headquarters tomorrow," he replied. "And thank you. You have no idea what this will mean to everyone."

I nodded politely, unsure what to say. Trent was kind, but Jensen had been kind as well. Who knew when Trent would turn, or if he and the others would even have time to formulate a cure?

All thoughts were suddenly driven from my mind when I saw Avery bringing out some canned fruit, beans and chicken. We opened them quickly and ate about five cans each, downing them as quickly as we could. Cold, canned food had never been my favorite, but with everything that had happened in the last week, it tasted wonderful. Trent brought in some buckets of stream water that tasted amazingly cool and refreshing.

As I settled on my pile of blankets for the night, full and completely content for the first time since we'd left for the island, I realized I wasn't afraid anymore. Trent seemed quite calm and reasonable for a beast, a vivid contrast to the mutations I'd met so far. Avery even seemed less fiery under his calming presence. She'd even forgot to wear her gun holster, something she'd never removed once in the time I'd been in the Shadowlands.

And yet, Avery and Trent made two different beds for themselves, though they'd been married for who knew how long. They barely touched, barely recognized each other. Clearly, something happened between them, but I felt too tired to try and figure it out. As I listened to the sound of crickets chirping outside the cave walls, I drifted off into a comfortable sleep with Wes on the blanket beside me, his fingers gently entwined in mine.

As faint sunlight filled the cracks in the ceiling and filtered down, I woke and sat up. Wes still slept deeply, his eyebrows furrowed, a frown creasing his lips. Avery slept in the bed in the alcove, her body curled unnaturally tightly. Trent slept across the room on another pallet, his head on his arms, his knees tucked into his chest.

I looked closer, startled to notice a sort of change in him. His skin, so markedly pale yesterday, had a slight, colorful tinge to it. Maybe it was my eyes playing tricks, but he seemed less…beastly.

I laid back down, still tired but unable to sleep anymore. A half-hour or so went by as I dozed in and out of consciousness, until finally everybody woke up. Avery gathered some more cans for a hasty breakfast, which we all scarfed down again.

I noticed that Avery glanced at Trent a couple times, an unbelieving look on her face. As she handed the cans to Trent to take to her makeshift garbage out in the back of the cave, I sidled up to her.

"Did you notice a change in Trent too?" I asked. She glanced at me, visibly startled.

"Yes," she replied, her eyebrows rising high. "He seems less…beastly."

"I saw it too, but I don't know what might have caused it."

I glanced around the room, trying to find something that might have caused such a stark change. Only Avery's dried herbs, canned food, cooking pot and other miscellaneous items sat scattered around. I noticed my bag that I'd taken with me from the city sitting near his pallet, but other than that, everything seemed ordinary and normal.

On a hunch, I walked to the pallet and picked up my bag. I sifted through it, not finding anything but some plastic food wrappers and Wes's dried bouquet. The flowers had long since withered and faded, the stems brittle, yet it still held a slight fragrance.

I noted the lilies and the greens, but a few stalks of some kind of purple flower looked unfamiliar. I tried and tried to figure out why they looked so familiar when it suddenly hit me like a ton of bricks. They were heather, the same plant that cleaned the soil in the north.

I separated one of the stalks from the bunch, staring at it wonderingly. As I walked back to Avery with the little flower in my hand, she gave me a strange look.

"Where'd you get the heather?" she asked, taking the little stalk from me and looking at it closely.

"It was in my bag, in a bouquet from Wes. What can heather do?"

"What do you mean?"

"I mean, does it have medicinal properties?"

She looked at it carefully. "This variety is particularly known for its calming properties, but it can also be used for raising low blood pressure and clearing up minor cuts and abrasions."

Suddenly, she looked up at me, her eyes wide. "You don't think…"

"That heather can help ease the effects of Akrium?"

She nodded, a look of hopeful excitement on her face. "Yes! Do you think this might be part of the cure?"

I didn't answer because Trent came in at that moment. He stretched a little and looked at us, clearly confused by our sudden excitement and interest.

"What?" he asked, looking at us warily.

"Trent, how do you feel this morning?" asked Avery.

He looked at her and shrugged. "I don't know," he replied, looking at us uncomfortably. "What do you mean?"

"I mean," said Avery impatiently, "your…problems. With being a mutant and all."

He rolled his eyes. "Gee, thanks."

"I don't mean it in a mean way," she cried, exasperated. "I mean, do you feel any better?"

He gave her a funny look, as if trying to recall something. "Well…the Akrium makes your blood vessels in the brain swell, so I usually have at least a dull headache, but it's not there today."

He looked at her expectantly, but Avery had turned her gaze towards me. "This is it!" she whispered excitedly. "This is part of the cure!"

Chapter Twenty-Nine
Lily

I looked down at the sprigs in my hand, feeling slightly skeptical. Avery noticed, and hurriedly added, "Of course it isn't the whole cure, but I think it has something to do with it!"

Trent looked at us questioningly. "The heather," I offered. "We think it might ease some of the symptoms."

He stood there, looking unimpressed. "Yeah, we figured that out a long time ago. We've been working with different herbs for years, seeing if anything would cure us. So far, heather and lavender are the only things that ease the symptoms, but they can't fully cure the disease. That's where you come in, Lily."

A sick feeling crept into the pit of my stomach at the thought of being a "cure" again. I'd already felt enough like a freak from the moment I found out what I really was, but the fact that everyone wanted to study me was almost more than I could bear.

"Look...what exactly are you going to do?" I asked hesitantly. "About this whole cure thing?"

Trent looked at me carefully, seeming guarded. I wondered if he were making up a lie to tell. "Just like I told you. We'll take a DNA sample, probably a saliva sample, and compare your DNA with ours."

"And...it's as simple as that?"

"Well, from there, we'll have to synthesize your type of DNA using specialized equipment. I have a feeling that all our equipment is a bit out of date. We'll have to do another raid."

"Raid? As in what you did at the Mainframe a couple months ago?"

He grimaced. "Yeah...I remember that. We've had to periodically raid to get supplies that we needed for testing. We have a network of spies in the city as well, so we can figure out what the Mainframe is up to and try to stop any further injections. So far, we haven't been very successful."

He sighed a little, his shoulders slumping from some invisible weight. "We have the equipment to analyze DNA. We got that when we found out about you."

My heart began to race again, refusing to calm even when Wes took my hand in his. I hadn't noticed him edge across the room towards me until now.

"How…did you find out about me?"

"Our spies. Vic's been looking for you for some time, but had a little trouble because your mother covered her tracks well. She always stayed off the radar, never drawing attention to herself, but some investigation at the hospital apparently helped them find you. She couldn't really help getting sick."

As the awful truth fell into place, I sank down on a nearby stone. I'd been followed all my life, and doing what I'd done to save mom had put a big red target on my forehead. I might as well have jumped up and down in front of the Mainframe screaming, "I'm your freak! Come get me!"

I'd never realized or fully appreciated mom's efforts to keep me safe. All her weird habits suddenly made sense, her whisking me away after winning big track races at school, the constant switches from job to job, accompanied by the endless moves all over the city…it finally all made sense. And even now, she might be in peril from the Mainframe. Tears formed in my eyes as I thought of how I'd endangered myself and ultimately her.

"Lily?" I looked up at Wes, but even he couldn't comfort me now. All I could do was hope that they hadn't found her. How could I have let things get so bad? I should have been trying to rescue her from day one.

And yet…

The idea came so subtly that I might have missed it if my mind hadn't caught hold of it. I'd always been fair at negotiating. Maybe the beasts would negotiate now.

"Trent, are you still sending in spies?"

"Yeah. We have to. It's the only way we can keep up with what's going on."

"My mom might be in danger. Is there any way you can find out if she's being held in the Mainframe, or Biltmore?"

"The Mainframe is definitely possible, but I don't know about Biltmore. It's pretty heavily guarded."

"Please, Trent," I begged, "I need to find out what happened to her. As soon as I disappeared, I'm sure they hauled her in for questioning. I'll do *anything* you want if you'll just help me find her."

Trent raised his eyebrows, considering. Wes's hand clamped firmly on my shoulder.

"Lily, do you really want to do this?" he muttered under his breath. "Remember what happened the last time you made a deal?"

"This isn't like last time, Wes. I hold the upper hand here. Besides, I have you to protect me,"

"I'll see what I can do," Trent offered. "I can't guarantee anything, but some of our guys, me included, were trained in genetic alteration. I can see if they can do a good enough disguise and steal some guard clothes to get in or something."

"Thank you," I replied.

"It might take a while, though, and we'd really like to at least look at your DNA." He looked at me, hope and fear raging in his mutated eyes.

"Well…we have nothing else to do today." I stood up and squeezed Wes's hand reassuringly. He pulled me closer and put his arm around me, as if to let Trent and Avery know he intended to keep his promise about protecting me. It was a little cheesy, but I appreciated his gesture all the same.

We left the cave soon after and started the long trek through the woods. As we walked, I noticed some things I'd seen yesterday and felt a surge of reassurance that the woods had become familiar to me.

Before long, we came to a clearing. Trent led us through the open space to a small, naturally-made tunnel of trees. The trunks crowded close together, making the going a little tricky.

"Wait a minute," Trent said, holding us back with his arm. He walked forward into the little tunnel, covering his mouth with a handkerchief. He sprayed some kind of mist from a small bottle he pulled from his pocket, then waved us on.

"What was that all about?" Wes asked as we hunched down and crawled through the tunnel.

"I had to get rid of our protective measures for a minute," he replied. I noticed he'd hung back, waiting for us all to go through. Then he took out another bottle and sprayed it around the entrance before following. "We've made a spray of various hallucinogenic and poisonous plants. When inhaled, it can create feelings of hysteria and fear. It keeps intruders away. The other spray neutralizes the harmful fumes."

"He really does talk like a science nerd, doesn't he?" Wes muttered with a grin. I smiled back, chuckling a little. For all his beastliness, Trent really did kind of sound like a human dictionary.

At the end of the tunnel, we found a small opening in the side of a massive cliff. As before, Trent held us back as he went ahead to spray, then motioned us to follow.

"I'm sorry for the precautions, but we have to be careful. The last thing we need is the idiots at the Mainframe shutting us down."

"I wouldn't worry about that," I replied. "They're afraid of you. Nobody even wants to go into the woods anymore."

He chuckled a little, making him look scarier than ever. I took Wes's hand as we crawled through the opening. The little tunnel finally widened out until we could stand. Trent led us through a series of winding rock tunnels, seemingly leading to nowhere. As we continued, I tried to fight off the eerie feeling that Trent might be leading us into a trap. However, as we rounded yet another bend, a gasp of amazement escaped me. I couldn't help being impressed with what I saw.

The last tunnel had taken us to a huge, open cavern. In one section of the room, a couple beasts sat poring over documents and talking quickly in their raspy voices. Other beasts stood gathered together, some even female, talking about something in low voices. Some sat under some huge screens with headphones on, apparently jabbering at someone on the other end of the communication device. Against the wall stood several tables with vials, different plant leaves and other chemicals. I had to hand it to them. They'd managed to make a home and a laboratory, despite their circumstances.

All the chatter died away as we entered the large room. Everyone dropped whatever work they had to stare at us. One particularly tall beast, standing in the middle of the larger crowd of beasts, walked forward with gleaming eyes.

"You got the girl?"

"Yes, Lycus, but…"

"Donovan!" he walked over to where we stood, leering in my direction. "Didn't think you had it in you! But you got her after all."

The tall beast clapped Trent on the back, but his eyes never left me. The same kind of frightening hunger I'd seen in Vic's eyes was mirrored in this man's. I backed away instinctively, fighting the urge to run.

"Lycus, back off," Trent said sternly, his raspy voice sounding even more ominous as it echoed around the room. "We're doing DNA testing, and that's it."

"You're taking a swab and letting her go?" Lycus rasped. "Why on *earth* would you do that?"

That decided it. I definitely didn't like Lycus, with his cold sneering face and harsh manner. I backed away even more, feeling Wes's hand clamp more tightly around mine.

"You're not in charge here, Lycus, I am. You'll do as I say and leave the girl alone, is that clear?"

Trent's willingness to protect me comforted me, but I felt a ripple of annoyance. I did have a name, and yet everyone referred to me as "The Girl."

"Her *name* is Lily," Wes grunted, as if he'd read my thoughts. I smiled at him, and he tried to smile back, but didn't manage much more than a half-hearted grin. I could almost hear his brain whirring at high speed, trying to figure out how to get us out of here.

Before either of us could do anything, Trent turned to us. "I'll keep everyone away, don't worry. Just follow me over here, please."

We slowly walked to where he pointed, both of us nervous. Even Avery seemed nervous, despite the fact that Trent clearly was in charge, as he'd said. From a makeshift wooden cabinet, he took some long cotton swabs and plastic gloves.

"Stay here," he commanded. He walked across the room to grab a small flashlight off of a table. The beasts watched his every move carefully. The quiet in the room was beginning to unnerve me. I wished they'd all go back to whatever they were doing instead of staring at us.

"Right, open wide." I jumped, not noticing that Trent had come up right next to me. I opened my mouth slowly, then shut it.

"Hang on," I said. "How do I know that you didn't lace these swabs with something while my back was turned?"

Trent gave a low laugh that sounded like a bark. "Didn't I just get everyone away from you? I've kept my end of the deal so far. Why would I ruin whatever chance we have to get a cure by poisoning you?"

Though uneasy, I slowly opened my mouth, then shut it again. Trent just laughed lightly and shook his head.

"You definitely don't trust me, do you?"

"Not really. Sorry."

"Tell you what," he started, walking over to the same wooden cabinet, "why don't I get a different swab? That way you know for sure I haven't poisoned it."

"Fair enough," I replied. I watched him carefully, but he didn't seem to be doing anything to the swab. He brought it right over and held it under my nose.

"You'd be able to smell something if I'd put poison on it. See?"

The swab was odorless. I opened my mouth once again, and fought hard against the instinct to shut it. Trent took a quick sample, stored it in a container, and rushed over to another table, directly beneath the huge screens. We followed, somewhat awkwardly, but Trent didn't seem worried about us right then.

"Creet! Samuels! Come help me with this!"

Two beasts pushed their way through the crowd until they'd come to Trent's side. One took the sample, unscrewed the bottle and waved the tip under some kind of scanner. Then he handed it to the other beast, who grabbed a container of clear fluid and swished the swab around in it. As the liquid began to change to a light, greenish color, he added some kind of chemical, stirred once more, then swabbed a bit on some kind of screen.

"Sheldon, we need you too," Trent shouted to the crowd at large. Another beast, far more sickly looking than the others, came to Trent's side. Trent whispered something to him and the beast opened his mouth. Trent took a swab, just as he'd done with me, then repeated the same procedure with Creet and Samuels.

A few moments later, two large, complicated-looking images popped up on the screens. Both showed microscopic images of DNA. I could just make out the faint, double helix pattern, but the strands showed some kind of blotchy mark along the sides of the helix on one of the images that seemed to have caused a break in the actual genetic material. The other looked much the same, but instead of fuzzy edges, the blotches were smooth and the DNA remained intact.

Trent and the others gazed up at the images, transfixed. Finally, he looked at the others, excited. "This is it!" he cried. "This is the answer we've been waiting for!"

"Good," drawled Lycus. I glanced over at him and felt my heart rate pick up in alarm. He glared at me. "Now we can get rid of all of them. We can't possibly let them get out and start telling everyone what we're up to."

Chapter Thirty
Elaine

Elaine leaned against the cold wall of her cell, starving and weak. The long week had passed slowly, but was nearing an end. She'd still refused to talk, and Vic and his cronies were growing impatient with her. Aggs had fed Elaine as well as she could, sneaking scraps from meals and handing them to her through the bars when she came back, but it wasn't enough.

They'd become fast friends, swapping stories of years past. Aggs had hugged her as Elaine told her through tears of her husbands' injection and subsequent disappearance.

In return for Aggs' kindness, Elaine had kept Aggs as warm as possible, tearing stuffing out of her mattress and throwing together a makeshift quilt with the sheet. Elaine slept blanketless on a bare mattress, but she didn't mind. She felt it was the least she could do for the poor woman. Though Elaine heaped Aggs with as many homemade blankets or other items as she could scrounge up, Aggs still shivered violently and coughed. Though Elaine hated the thought, she knew Aggs wasn't much longer for this life. The colder weather didn't help, either. As fall crept in, Elaine found herself longing for the dreadfully hot and humid summer days.

As Elaine woke one morning, she saw the same cruel guard standing before her door. He leered at her, flexing his whip menacingly.

"Judgment day," he cackled, his voice full of an awful triumph. He opened her cell and led her out, down the hall and to the lobby. Vic stood there, a sour look on his face.

"Are you ready to talk yet?" he barked, clearly angry. His normally smooth hair sat disheveled across his forehead, hanging down in greasy strings. Stubble spread across his face, giving him a five o'clock shadow though it was morning.

Elaine predictably stood stubbornly with her mouth tightly closed, bracing herself for whatever they planned to do.

"Take her to the dungeon," Vic snapped at the guard.

"With pleasure," the cruel man replied.

They led Elaine off to another hallway. The "dungeon" as they'd put it, turned out to be a dark, windowless room off the hall, far removed from any of the main rooms. Vic removed the manacles from her wrists that the guard had placed there to move her from her cell.

"Elaine, this is enough. I've tried everything to be kind, but you're testing my patience. Now, has Lily been in contact with you?"

Despite the awful existence Elaine had endured, a snicker escaped her throat. "How can she be in touch with me? I'm in jail!"

She started to laugh hysterically, realizing with a sudden jolt that she was bordering insanity.

"I know, you idiot!" Vic screamed, looking positively manic. "Do you know where your daughter is?" She stayed silent as she'd been so accustomed to doing.

"Bring out the whip," he muttered. Before Elaine could move or react, a stinging stripe slashed across her back, making her scream out in pain.

"Ah, she speaks!" Vic snarled, glaring at her with intense hatred. "Now, tell me what you know about your daughter's whereabouts!"

She didn't answer and felt the agony of the whip again. The second cut hurt slightly less than the first since she knew it would come, but it was far from pleasant. She managed only a slight whimper this time.

Again and again it continued for what felt like an hour, her refusal to talk and subsequent whippings. Her clothes soon hung tattered against her back, shredded and covered in blood. Tears streamed down her face, but she didn't sob or break down like he expected her to. She clenched her fists so hard that the manicured tips dug into her palms, making them bleed as well. Vic finally gave up, realizing that she did not intend to talk. He gave the sign to stop, then approached Elaine.

"You've made your choice, then," he growled, his putrid breath making her already nauseous stomach churn. "Another week with no food."

He shoved Elaine roughly towards the guard, who clenched his huge, meaty fist around her arm and practically dragged her through the halls. As they approached her cell, he threw open the door and shoved her inside.

Without a word, he strode away. She sat up, fully sobbing now as the pain seared across her raw back.

"Elaine? What happened?" said Aggs's haggard voice from the neighboring cell. Elaine crawled over to her, too weak to talk, and collapsed near the bars. She heard Aggs' sharp intake of breath, her angry muttering, and felt something cool across her back. She blacked out, diving into the welcome relief from the pain.

As Elaine came to, she realized evening had fallen. She sat up and looked around blearily. Aggs sat next to her, a worried frown creasing her face.

"What did they do to you?" she whispered, tears spilling from her faded brown eyes.

"They need information on Lily, and I refused to tell them anything," Elaine replied, her voice hoarse from disuse. How long had she been out?

As if she'd read Elaine's mind, Aggs told her she'd been asleep for nearly a whole day. Aggs had been applying wet rags to Elaine's skin and cleaning it as best she could, but without new clothing or bandages to dress the wounds, things looked pretty bleak.

"I have some food. Are you hungry?"

The time had passed for shame or manners. Elaine took the small roll and handful of beans she offered and wolfed them down, but the meager rations barely sated her. She lay down on her stomach, hungry but mostly thirsty, her back aching in a never ending crescendo of pain. Aggs stroked Elaine's hair and sang softly to her some song she'd never heard until she fell asleep again.

When Elaine woke again later, she felt a little better, but still exhausted. Aggs had managed to smuggle a cup of water in with her, which she drank gratefully. Elaine wiped her parched lips and looked up into Aggs' wrinkled face.

"Aggs, you've got to stop doing this," she mumbled. "I'll get you in trouble."

"Nonsense. They won't treat another human being like this under my watch."

Elaine sat up, a little dizzy but feeling more able to than she had before. "Thank you…for everything. I don't know what I'd do without you."

"Well, you've helped me too," she replied with a withered smile. "It's nice to have someone to talk to."

Elaine managed a weak smile back before she fell against the mattress again. She wanted to stay awake, to talk to Aggs some more, but the exhaustion and dull pain overtook her again.

Elaine woke again, this time in the middle of the night. Something was wrong, very wrong. She looked around, wondering why she felt so off, when she realized she no longer heard Aggs's soft singing or felt her gnarled fingers gently stroking her hair. Elaine stood up a little too quickly and sagged against the bars, but she noticed Aggs was not in her cell. She crawled over to the bars that faced the hall and whispered hoarsely to try and get the attention of the woman across from her. The woman finally sat up, the sight of her grotesque face and frizzy red hair making Elaine jump slightly.

"What?" she said loudly, then emitted a large belch.

"What happened to Aggs?"

"Don't talk so loud!" she bellowed. Elaine rolled her eyes. This was the drunk Aggs had told her about, the one who'd found a way to pay of a guard to smuggle her in liquor every now and again.

"D'you mean the old hag over there?" she grumbled, pointing vaguely in the wrong direction. Elaine stifled the angry things she wanted to say to this awful woman and nodded.

"They packed her up and shipped her off. She's gone to another cell."

Elaine sagged once more against the bars, her strength completely gone. She realized they must have caught on, must have figured out that Aggs had helped her, and any punishment they forced her to endure was now her fault. Elaine began to sob uncontrollably, sliding down the bars and landing in a heap on the floor. Her one beacon of light in this horrible place, her one last respite, was gone.

Chapter Thirty-One
Elaine

"Up you get, lady," came the gruff voice of Elaine's hated guard. She opened her eyes blearily to see him standing there, whip in hand. "We've gotta get you prettied up for your court appearance."

He grinned evilly and unlocked her door. Once again, she was led through the long corridor back to the main lobby and found Vic looking at her, a sneer of triumph on his face.

"Well, well, well...here we are!" he said. "Trial day!"

Elaine stared at him unbelievingly. "What?"

"You didn't think we were complete tyrants, did you? You still have the right to a trial. It's just been...pushed back. Several times."

Before Elaine could respond, a harsh looking woman took her by the arm and led her to a nearby washing room. The woman sat Elaine back in a chair and roughly washed her hair, dried it with a dryer and brushed some quick makeup over her face.

"Change into this," the woman said, wrinkling her nose at the dirty, disgusting state of Elaine's ugly prison jumper. She handed Elaine a soft black skirt suit with a plain white blouse to go underneath the jacket. Elaine headed for a stall and changed quickly, trying to figure out what on earth was going on.

After she finished, the woman led her back to Vic and handed her over to the custody of the guard with the whip. They walked out to a car and once more drove the short distance to the Mainframe. Instead of going up into the offices, as they'd done on previous visits, they went right to the large, lavish courtroom on the first floor.

A full breakfast stood on a table with platters of eggs, meats and other delicacies that most definitely weren't available to the general public. Elaine stood back, knowing Vic still wanted to starve her and keep her beaten down. She wouldn't take his bait.

A woman approached Elaine, some kind of court recorder by the looks of it. "Would you like some of these buns? They're delicious," she said shyly. Clearly, she didn't realize Elaine was on trial. Or maybe she did. Elaine couldn't tell anymore what was happening around her and suddenly didn't care.

Hesitantly, she took a sugary roll and took a bite of the soft bread. It took all her self-restraint not to gobble it down quickly and reach for another. The kind woman offered some more food and Elaine took it gratefully, glad that the public setting seemed to restrain Vic from his torture.

Elaine was led to a small chair behind a desk while Vic bustled off to talk to some men in the jury box. Most of them looked at her coldly as Vic talked, while others tried to hide their clear feelings of sympathy. The judge walked in a short time later and took his seat. He shot Elaine a furtive look and sighed. She wondered if it was her imagination, but he seemed to have pity for her already.

After all the formalities of court, the judge sat up straight and looked down at her. "Miss Mitchell, you've been charged with high treason in aiding and abetting one Lily Mitchell, a known criminal. For your crimes, you appear here on trial today. How do you plead?"

Elaine looked around, terrified, not knowing who might help her or even care about her situation.

"I'm not going to deny that I will protect my daughter against any odds, but-"

"You see there? Clearly guilty," said Vic, a self-satisfied grin plastered across his greasy face. Elaine noticed he'd combed his hair again and didn't look as haggard as he had before.

"President, will you please hold your peace," the judge replied in a bored tone. "As there are no witnesses to present, we will proceed to the jury after President Channing presents his case."

Vic got up and gloatingly laid out all the evidence against Elaine, saying that she'd engineered a way to help Lily escape and get rid of the tracking bug. He claimed she'd hindered the war effort and justice itself, making it impossible to obtain a vital addition to the army. She clenched her fists angrily, but how could she stand up for herself? Vic surely had the whole thing rigged and was just doing the trial to look like a saint.

"As law dictates, Mr. President, the jury will decide," said the judge. He looked straight at them, almost pleadingly. "I would advise the jury to think carefully about the consequences of their actions."

A few laughed outright at the strange, cryptic message from the judge, but one or two looked at Elaine again, a strange sort of acknowledgement in their eyes.

For an hour, the jury convened, making the decision. She sat, twitching nervously, her now-satisfied stomach churning loudly as it processed the food it hadn't had in so long.

At last they emerged from the small chamber off the main room, some looking downright angry as they took their seats, but most of them looking smug. One of them took the sentence to the judge, who read it silently to himself with a frown.

He sighed deeply, then stood.

"Elaine Mitchell, the court finds you guilty of high treason. Your sentence, to be carried out one week from now, is death."

Chapter Thirty-Two
Lily

"Lycus!" thundered Trent. "You won't touch her! I know you're angry, but get over it already! She's agreed to help us!"

I looked from the terrifying beast to my right to Trent at the table, confused.

"What do you mean?" I asked nervously.

Lycus, glaring at me, didn't answer. Instead, he took the sleeve of his ragged shirt and pulled it up over his shoulder. A glaring wound, scabbed over but still nasty, spread across his shoulder. I hadn't noticed before, but he didn't use his left arm much. Now as I saw the wound, his strange movements suddenly made sense.

"You're the one that..."

I trailed off, horrified. "Yes," he sneered. "I'm the one that you shot that day at the Mainframe. Without medicine or proper equipment, it takes a lot longer to heal, and my bones are permanently damaged. Thanks to *you*."

"It was an accident, I was scared," I replied. "The Mainframe caught me, and-"

"Spare me the sob story," Lycus shot back. "Unfortunately, I can't kill you because of soft-hearted Donovan, but mark my words, I'll get even."

He stalked off through the crowd to some tunnel branching off from the main room. I looked at Wes, who stood with his teeth clenched, his hands balled into fists.

"Don't listen to that idiot," Wes muttered. "I won't let anything happen to you."

Trent walked over from the table. "I'm sorry," he said, his hands out in sort of a helpless gesture. "Lycus knows he's going off the deep end, and it's difficult on him. He was angry when we found you and you took off, and he's been raving about revenge to everyone who'll listen."

My heart sank. Lycus probably had several others on his side, judging by the glares I got from some of the beasts in the room.

"I appreciate your coming," Trent continued, his eyes sincere even through all the red. "I've finally figured it out."

"Figured what out?"

"The missing link. What makes you immune." He couldn't help smiling triumphantly.

"What is it?" asked Avery as she sidled up next to us.

"Lily's DNA is different from any I've ever seen," he said, pointing towards the screen with the smooth blotches. "All the regular combinations of proteins exist in the cells, but I found an extra element, incredibly rare, which seems to automatically repair the breakage from the Akrium. Those fuzzy blotches are compounds in the Akrium that break down the DNA. Lily's blotches are smooth because they've been repaired by this element."

"Um…in English?" I asked.

"I think," he began excitedly, "and this is just a theory, but I think that your mother passed on this dormant gene to you, one that gives extraordinary adrenaline, much more than an ordinary person. In times when endurance would originally be used, as in exercise, you produce more adrenaline, making you faster and stronger than normal people."

"But I thought that was attributed to the Akrium in me," I replied.

"Yes, it is, partly. But this gene feeds on the good qualities of Akrium and somehow overrides the bad. I'm not sure exactly how it happens, but this is the answer! It's the cure!"

"What is? Mating with people who aren't injected with Akrium to make a healthy generation?" Avery asked, looking skeptical.

"No," Trent replied. "We need to replicate this gene, synthesize it, and inject ourselves with it. My theory is that the gene will begin to repair our broken DNA strands and cure us."

"So…that's it? You've found it?"

"I still need to test it," he replied. "But I'm pretty sure this is the only thing we've found that gives us any hope. But we're going to need a lot of equipment. I don't have anything that will help us synthesize genes. We'll have to make another raid on the Mainframe, but it'll be a big haul. We'll need trucks, and probably all of us will need to be there to overwhelm them…"

He trailed off, lost in his own little world, as he walked back to the table with the huge screens. Still mumbling to himself, he began to take notes on a pad of paper. After a while, he started directing other beasts around, giving instructions and watching as they ran off to fulfill them. It looked as though he planned to start the raid immediately.

I sat down on a nearby rock, feeling a overwhelmed and a little worried. Trent seemed to have forgotten the promise he made me about mom, but how could I mention it here in this atmosphere of mingled elation and hostility? Though Trent felt sure he'd found a cure, I could tell from the looks on many of the other's faces that they felt skeptical.

"Well…do you guys want to go back to the cave?" Avery asked.

"Yeah, but are we allowed to?" I asked. "And besides, even if we wanted to, we need someone to spray and get rid of the poison around the entrances."

"I'll talk to Trent. Maybe he can take you two again, or one of the others."

I looked up sharply. "You're staying here?"

She shrugged. "I feel like I should, but I don't really know why. Trent's obsessed with finding a cure."

I noticed for the first time just how drawn and pale she looked. "Avery…is everything ok? With you and Trent?"

Her face darkened. "I thought he'd be glad to see me, but since I've been here, all he's asked about is how to find you so that he could do the DNA test. Like I say, nothing matters to him anymore except finding a cure, not even his family. I think this lot's mania finally got to him."

"Well…" I didn't know what to say to comfort her. "He said he started working on a cure so he could get back to you, didn't he?"

"Yeah, it may have started that way, but he's always been this way. You should have seen him when his group discovered Akrium. It's all he talked about, and when he disappeared-"

She cut herself off abruptly and frowned. "I'm sorry. I shouldn't be talking about this."

"Why?"

"I don't know. I feel a little ungrateful, especially since I've found what I'm looking for. I don't know why I thought I could just bring him home. Of course he'd want to be normal first."

She looked over at me, her eyes full of conflict. "I'll see what I can do to get you back to the cave."

With that, she walked slowly over to Trent, but he waved her off, still trying to make notes. She shrugged, and came to sit next to Wes and I, her shoulders slumped. I didn't say anything, and neither did she, so we sat in awkward silence as the beasts finally shuffled back to whatever they'd been doing before we came.

The day passed agonizingly slowly as the beasts conferred with Trent about his studies. He rarely left the table with the screens, leaving only to gather some herbs from another nearby table, or talk to the beasts who sat studying papers.

Finally, a random beast approached us with some hard, clearly homemade bread and a can of beans each. "Thought you all might be hungry," he grunted, then left. The bread tasted like ground up bark, which probably was how they made their flour. The beans were cold, but otherwise tasted fine.

"Why don't we just go?" Wes whispered at one point. "I hate feeling like everyone is watching us, waiting to kill us or something."

"I know," I whispered back. "And I've breathed in those poisons before, they're really not that bad. They just take a while to wear off. Maybe we could get through them."

Avery looked wearily at her watch. "Let's just wait a little longer. Trent's bound to take a break sometime."

I felt a sudden awful pang of pity for Avery. She hadn't eaten much, and kept her eyes mostly on Trent. It reminded me of a small child I'd seen once on the street, watching each adult that passed carefully, her large eyes pleading for a scrap of something. I'd given her the few coins I had, not being much better off myself, and her whole expression changed in a split second. She'd lit up like a candle and run off, excited to be able to help her mother and younger siblings. Avery seemed much the same, just waiting for Trent to take notice.

Suddenly angry, I stood up.

"Um…what are you doing?" Wes asked.

"Something," I replied. I marched over to Trent and tapped him. He turned, gave a vague smile, then turned back to his work.

"Trent," I said loudly over the talk of beasts. "You need to listen to me."

"Not now," he replied. "I think I've figured out-"

I yanked him away from the table by the arm before he could finish. He looked at me, startled.

"You need to listen," I started, feeling a little nervous. "Avery has been waiting over a year to see you, and you've blown her off just because you want a cure."

"Hey, what-"

"She brought a cure to you, and you've pretty much ignored her this whole time," I interrupted. "She needs you more than ever. The cure can wait."

"But-"

"It can wait," I repeated. "Besides, you made a promise to me too. My mother could be in danger. I held up my end of the deal. It's your turn to hold up your end."

His face hardened, making him look more beastly than ever. I stepped back a little, trying to keep my cool, but he definitely scared me.

"You know I'm right," I said, sounding much bolder than I felt. For a second, he looked as if he wanted to get angrier, but thought better of it. His eyes slowly softened.

"I'm sorry," he replied. "I've just been worried. We're losing more men every day, and I can feel myself going sometimes. I've been lucky that my disease has progressed this slowly, but…"

"If you've lasted this long, you can last a little longer. Spend some time with your wife. Involve her in the cure. She knows more about herbs and natural cures than anyone I've ever met."

His eyes suddenly lit up with interest. "That's true…I forgot about that book she has. I'll bet she can find-"

"First, just spend some time with her," I interrupted again. "And please send someone to find out what's going on with my mom."

He smiled and motioned me to follow him. He walked over to the table with beasts wearing headsets and tapped one on the shoulder. After a whispered conversation, he turned to me.

"Yaris is on it now," he said. "As it is, we still have men there getting some other information we need. I had to relay some information anyway, so I asked Yaris to relay the information about your mother."

The man with the headset looked up at us. "Laherty says he's on it. Might take a day or two, but he'll check the Mainframe for any prisoners, and if he can't find her there, he'll try getting in at Biltmore."

A tremendous wave of relief rushed over me. "Thank you. Her name is Elaine Mitchell."

Trent related the information to Yaris, who repeated it into the small microphone in the headset. He nodded affirmatively, then went back to whatever research he'd been working on.

We walked back to Wes and Avery. She seemed surprised, and looked at me a little suspiciously.

"I'm sorry, Ave," Trent said as he took her hand. "We have a lot to talk about, and I got caught up in everything else."

She stood up and looked at him warily, clearly still unsure if she could believe him. Trent smiled down at her, seeming to notice her for the first time. Then, as if remembering something, he looked at Wes and I.

"You're both probably tired, and hungry," he said. "We don't have the greatest provisions, but I can get you some of our dry goods and a room."

"That would be great," I replied. I noticed a lot of the beasts were putting down their equipment or papers and stretching out, clearly ready to quit for the night. Trent took us into one of the winding passages leading off the main room. The tunnel ended in a small crawlspace with a few blankets laid out on the floor.

"It's not the best, but the blankets are thick and warm. If you need anything, I'll…um, *we'll* be in the main room."

"Thanks."

Trent took Avery's hand again and they left. I felt relieved to finally have a little privacy, but it didn't last long. A lanky looking man who seemed in the beginning stages of decay brought us some undercooked rice and more beans. We ate quickly, then fell on the blankets. I was so tired I didn't have time or energy to feel awkward about the fact that Wes and I were in a room, on a makeshift bed, alone. I drifted off immediately to sleep on the uncomfortable floor.

I'd only been asleep for what felt like five minutes when I terrifying roar ripped through the passage, waking us both.

Chapter Thirty-Three
Lily

"If she stays alive, Vic and his cronies will find her eventually," came a rough voice. He sounded a lot like Lycus, but I couldn't tell for sure. "You can still get more of her DNA after she's dead."

"You're out of your mind!" roared another voice that I recognized as Trent. "Leave her alone!"

I sat up and found Wes looking at me. Without a word, he grabbed my hand and pulled me up, searching for a way out of the twisting passages.

"Wait!" I said, balking my feet. "Lycus is coming through one of these tunnels. He knows the way better than we do. He might catch us."

"We've got to get out of here. We're causing a riot," he replied.

"If we run headlong into him, he'll probably kill us on the spot!" I tried to pull him back, but he leaned away from me, trying to look down the hall. Someone suddenly grabbed me from behind and whirled me around. Wes lifted his fists, ready to strike out.

"It's me," Trent hissed. "Things aren't good right now. Everybody is starting to side with Lycus, you've gotta get out of here."

"But what about…"

"We just got word from one of our comrades posted as night guard at Biltmore," he replied. "Your mom's there, she was sentenced to death just today."

"WHAT?" I shouted, cut off as Trent clapped a hand over my mouth.

"You've just got to leave, I don't know how much longer I can hold Lycus off." He slipped a small bottle into my hand. "Use this on the entrance and get out of here. Go to Avery's cave. I'll send two of our guys when I can. They'll take you to the city to get your mom."

"But it might be too late by the time…"

"It's my priority, don't worry," he replied. "Now go! Take the tunnel to the left, it loops the long way to the main room. And remember Heather."

I wondered what his cryptic message meant, but I didn't have time to figure it out. Wes grabbed my hand and tugged me through the tunnel, both of us feeling along the rough walls. At last, we broke into the dim light of the large cavern. It now sat eerily empty and quiet. We raced for the exit when another hideous roar erupted behind us. Lycus flew from a tunnel and ran straight for me, but Trent appeared from another tunnel and grabbed him from behind in a choke hold.

"GO!" he screamed.

We made it through the entrance as another roar sounded, followed by a loud shot. I stopped, shocked, and looked back.

"Was that-"

"No time to worry about it," Wes replied. "We've gotta move!"

Together we flew through the tunnel, pushing branches away and trying to see in the dark. Finally, I saw the mouth of the tunnel looming ahead and quickly took the spray out of my pocket. I didn't have time for more than two or three sprays. I knew immediately it wouldn't be enough.

I took a heavy, panting breath and started to feel terrible. My vision began to swim, and that same feeling of terror that had besieged me the first time I'd come to the forest stole over me again. I struggled to stay upright, losing Wes's hand in the chaos.

"Lily?" he choked. "Lily, where are you?"

I squinted, trying to see my way, and finally managed to grab his hand.

"They put something else in here," I gasped. "Something to make it hard to see. It wasn't like this at the entrance to the Shadowlands."

"What is it?"

"It's the chemicals that Trent talked about," I coughed. "They put it around the entrance to keep people away. I didn't have time to spray much of the antidote or whatever."

We kept walking, swaying dizzily, using the trees for support. My vision finally started to clear, and I could hear the stream once more.

"This way," I panted. Wes followed, his arms in front of him. The awful chemicals around the entrance must still be wearing off on him. I took his arm and guided him along until he could see.

The forest remained quiet as we followed the stream, until Avery's cave finally came into view. We stumbled into it as the sun started to rise through the trees. Exhausted, we collapsed immediately on the beds that still lay scattered around the cave.

When I woke, the cave lay in complete darkness. My stomach rumbled loudly, prompting me to get up and search for some food. As I looked in the cupboard, a pair of arms suddenly slipped around my waist. I took a sharp breath, surprised, then relaxed as I recognized Wes's touch. My heart sped up as he kissed the back of my neck lightly.

I turned to face him. His eyes surprised me, full of the humor and light he'd had before he'd been taken into the war. He kissed me, not a rushed, panic stricken kiss like the ones we'd experienced lately, but a kiss like those we used to share, one that took my breath and made me feel lightheaded.

"I just realized how…alone we are," he whispered huskily, sending shivers down my spine. I buried my face in his and wrapped my arms tightly around him, savoring the feeling of being with him again. It hit me suddenly, too, just how much I'd missed his fiery kisses, the comforting warmth of his arms.

"That we are," I whispered back, kissing him again.

He leaned his forehead against mine and brushed some stray hairs away from my forehead. I suddenly realized how bad I must have smelled, but then it didn't really matter. We'd both been through an absolute nightmare the past few months. We were lucky to be alive. Still, the girly part of me made me pat my hair self-consciously.

"Are you hungry?" I asked as my stomach rumbled again.

"Mmmmmm…" he replied suggestively. I stepped back and punched him playfully.

"Not *that* kind of hungry." I laughed and gently pulled away. Now was definitely not the time for that. I wanted to at least be showered first. Wes pouted, his lip out, but laughed when I told him his stinkiness was too much for me at the moment.

I turned back to the provisions and looked around. Luckily, Avery had some long-buried cans of preserves. The sugary fruit gave us some much needed energy, and we followed it with a drink of water from the stream. I noticed the moon high above the treetops. We'd slept for the whole day.

Suddenly footsteps sounded among the trees. I froze, terrified, listening intently. I could hear low, wheezing growls accompanying the footsteps. I took Wes's hand and pulled him carefully into the cave, trying not to make a sound.

"What's going on?" he whispered as soon as we got back to the main part of the cave.

"There are beasts out there," I replied.

We stayed quiet, hardly daring to breath, when one of them said something. He stood close by enough for us to hear through the crack in the wall.

"Is this the place?"

"I don't know," the other replied. "We could knock."

"You're really dumb, Jones."

I suddenly remembered Trent's promise to send the men out. "It's ok, Wes, they're the reinforcements."

I crept towards the entrance, but Wes held me back. "It might be a trap. How do we know we can really trust them?"

Chapter Thirty-Four
Lily

I shrugged. "I trust Trent, and I think he'll stick by his word. He got us out before Lycus could do anything."

"Well…let me go first," he whispered. He stepped outside and motioned me to follow. Two beasts stood near the stream looking around. They stopped when they saw Wes and backed away warily.

"Are you the two Trent sent?" I asked.

They nodded slowly, still looking slightly scared. "How do we know we can trust you?" Wes asked. One of them stepped forward hesitantly.

"Trent told us to tell you 'Heather.'" I remembered the strange instruction from Trent, and nodded. He must have used it for a password among those who were a little more together.

"We need your help too," the beast continued. "We're planning the final raid on the Mainframe. Trent tested the cure, and it worked."

He took out a flashlight and held it up near his eyes so we could see them. They glittered faintly, but didn't have the red tainted look of those suffering from full Akrium symptoms.

"But how do we know we can trust you?" he said suspiciously as he clicked the flashlight off. "You might turn us in."

I laughed in spite of the tension. "I'm sorry, it's just…why would I turn you in to someone that's after me too?"

The men seemed to relax a little after that. "I'm Jones, this is Barnwell," one of them said. They asked for some food since they'd been walking a good part of the day. I lighted a few candles while Wes dug up some beans for the men to eat. I noticed with dismay that Avery was now running short of food. I supposed she'd gone on raids of her own every now and then, but the supply she'd gathered the last time was dwindling fast. They drank some stream water after that, then sat down to rest a while.

"We've got to get going soon," said Barnwell, "but you'll need disguises."

They'd brought a bag of clothes with them. One outfit was a black Weatherall shirt and matching pants for Wes. They pulled out black spray dye and covered Wes's hair with it liberally. They also took out a small bottle and held it up.

"Eye dye," said Jones. "That way they can't identify you by eye color or on retinal scans. Just in case one of us is captured."

Wes took the dropper and put a few drops in each eye. When he finished, his hazel eyes had turned a dark brown. He was hardly recognizable. Then the beasts pulled out the same kind of black outfit for me, but streaked my hair with blonde instead of black. When I used the eye dye, my eyes turned a bright, turquoise blue. I looked at the beasts questioningly.

"It aligns with the color pigment of your eyes to create the exact opposite, or the most unrecognizable color," the man explained. "One of my best inventions."

"Wow," I replied. "It's incredible!"

I looked in a mirror and was shocked by the change. No one would recognize me now, except maybe my mom. We hurried to the entrance of the cave and out into the cold night. The Weatherall sleeves felt so much better than the white rags I'd been wearing previously.

Nobody talked much as we hiked through the woods towards the entrance to the Shadowlands. As we reached the familiar windy cave that led to the outside world, the beasts walked ahead of us and sprayed the anti-chemical solution around the outside walls. I shuddered slightly, remembering my awful encounter with that first beast. I randomly thought of Avery and wondered if she was okay. I didn't have long to wonder, however, because we got to the highway only to find ourselves in absolute chaos.

A huge line of cars ran along the highway, their drivers honking and cussing loudly. Jones held us back with an arm and put a finger to his lips. He motioned us to retreat farther into the trees.

"It'll look suspicious if we all come out at once," he whispered. He looked back at the scene before us and frowned. I looked at Wes. His face paled slightly as he looked at the sight. I longed to put my arms around him, but felt a little awkward with our escorts standing right there.

At long last, Jones turned back to us. "If I remember right, there's a frontage road near the beach. It looks like everyone is trying to get out of the city. It's probably not crowded like the highway. We'll head west and hit the frontage road and get to the city from there."

We followed obediently, all of us too nervous to talk. I took Wes's hand and squeezed it reassuringly, trying not to give in to the terror I felt. As Jones predicted, the frontage road was pretty empty.

"Split up and run," said Jones. "We'll meet up later in front of the Ration Center."

Before I had time to protest or ask if I could go with Wes, the two beasts took off. I looked at him searchingly.

"I guess it would be better if we split," he said quietly. "If they catch both of us, it could get bad."

I reached up and laced my fingers through his darkened hair and pulled him to me. He kissed me softly, his hands reaching around my waist.

"I love you," he murmured in my ear. He squeezed my hand one last time, then disappeared into the gathering gloom. Glad for the darkness, I started after him, then veered off to the right into a narrow alley. As I caught my breath, I noticed a woman sitting not far from me, worry creasing her eyes.

"Food to spare?" she croaked, her voice barely audible.

I shook my head. "Sorry."

I stepped lightly through the alley, trying to forget the woman's hollow eyes, her starved body. What happened here?

I reached the end and looked out cautiously. A few more shortcuts brought me to the street with the Ration Center, but I stopped cold as I approached the once familiar building. The sidewalks were lined with screaming people that led to a mob trying to break down the door. Some had succeeded in breaking windows and were crawling out of them, clutching packages of food with gleeful grins on their faces.

Frantically, I looked around for Wes and the others without trying to get in the middle of the mob. People pushed and swelled around me like the ebbing tide, making me dizzy.

At long last I spotted Barnwell trying to push through the mob towards me. I caught up with him and he pulled me to a safe spot between two buildings, away from the mayhem.

"Where are the others?" I shouted over the noise.

"Haven't seen them. It's a mess!"

"I know. Probably wasn't the best place to meet."

He took my arm once more and pushed us through the crowd, but before we could find anyone, a large rover rolled into the square. Nobody seemed to notice it, but I ducked as I recognized the Mainframe insignia emblazoned on its metal siding. I pulled Barnwell down with me as a heavy, yellow gas slowly descended on the crowd.

Chapter Thirty-Five
Lily

Coughing and gasping, we made our way through the crowd, trying to keep below the hovering poisonous cloud. Barnwell suddenly pushed something into my hand. He tried to tell me something, but the noise from the crowd made it impossible. He lifted a white, square cloth to his face and indicated I should do the same. I held up the cloth he gave me and noticed immediately that my head became a little less foggy. We pushed again through the crowd, one hand clutching the cloth to my face and the other holding Barnwell's hand.

We made it through the crowd into an obsolete alleyway where we could keep an eye out for the others. At long last, a familiar man stumbled to the edge of the crowd, coughing and wheezing.

"Jones!" shouted Barnwell. Jones stumbled towards the sound and reached us at last. His face blanched as he looked at the two of us.

"Where's Landon?" he gasped. "Wasn't he with you?"

He looked at me expectantly, but I couldn't talk. My mouth suddenly felt extremely dry. Barnwell stepped towards Jones, but his eyes scanned the crowd.

"We thought he was with you," he replied urgently.

"What's going on?" I finally found my voice.

"We have Akrium in our blood, things like Bleeding Gas don't affect us as much."

"Bleeding Gas?" I scanned the crowd again frantically. "What does that mean?"

"We worked with it in our original Akrium trials," said Barnwell wearily. "It makes your eyes bleed. It's only temporary, but it's enough to send a message if needed. Wes doesn't have Akrium infused in his genetic makeup, it'll hurt him worse."

Without thinking, I plunged towards the crowd again, despairing as I suddenly remembered that he was disguised. The noise from the people subsided slightly, but the gas had caused people to go into a panic. I kept my cloth on my face and searched frantically. The crowds finally cleared and I noticed a dark-haired man crouched on his knees. I ran to him and knelt beside him. I bit my tongue to keep from screaming as he looked up at me. His eyes, hazel again, were streaming blood profusely. With trembling hands, I took the handkerchief, trying to ignore the slight stinging in my eyes, and gently wiped the blood from his face.

"Lily?"

I nodded and pressed a finger to his lips. Barnwell and Jones suddenly appeared next to me and helped me lift him to his feet. Barnwell whipped a small vial from his pocket and dabbed some of the clear liquid in it on his handkerchief. He wiped Wes's eyes and they cleared.

"How did you…"

I trailed off, looking at Wes's now-clear eyes. Barnwell smiled grimly. "We worked for the Mainframe, remember? We know what to look for. But never mind, let's just get to Biltmore."

Wes laced his fingers through mine. "Thank you for finding me," Wes whispered. I didn't answer, but hugged him tightly to me. I couldn't quite shake the feeling of horror since I'd seen his eyes.

We trudged through the streets as dawn broke over the city, illuminating even more horror than the night before. People lay in the streets, starved to death or victims of some other gruesome end. Buildings lay in ruins, rubble scattered the streets.

"What happened?"

"The war. Channing. Starvation," muttered Jones. "The food shortage has driven everyone to insanity. Vic only cares about hunting for you now, and Epirus is finally striking back. All of our reinforcement has gone south to fight in the capitol there."

I looked around in disgust. The city had never been particularly beautiful, but the scene of carnage that met my eyes was too much. I'd still grown up here. It was my home, but now it lay in ruins.

We reached Biltmore just as the sun rose fully over the horizon. I shuddered, remembering my brief stay in the cold, damp cell. My heart squeezed painfully at the thought of my mother in there, probably starved and…the thought was too awful to finish.

"So…what's the plan?" I asked. "I've been in there. It's pretty heavily guarded."

"We've got a guy in there," said Barnwell. "We're meeting him."

We circled the building to the back, but nobody came to meet us. The building seemed shut tight, without the usual guards and other officials milling around the yard.

Suddenly, the doors banged open loudly and a few men hustled out. They carried something heavy between them and moved slowly.

"We've got to bury her quick. She's gotten too friendly with too many people. We'll have a riot on our hands," muttered one of the men. The other grabbed a large shovel and started plowing into the earth, digging as quickly as possible. A patch of long gray hair billowed over one of the men's arms. He turned suddenly and I caught a glimpse of her face.

"Aggs!"

Chapter Thirty-Six
Elaine

Elaine woke groggily, accustomed now to the feeling of dull hunger in her stomach and pain in her back. Vic had given her an awful beating for taking the food at the court. She rolled over, automatically trying to talk to Aggs, then pausing as she realized she was gone. Ever since they'd taken her a week ago, Elaine hadn't eaten, minus the rolls at the court.

She laid there for a while, trying to gather her strength, when a shout rose down the hallway. Elaine scooted over to the bars and clutched the metal to pull herself up.

"Janice!" she called weakly to the scary, frizzy-haired woman across the way. "Are you awake?"

No answer. She was probably still passed out from her haul last night. The woman really did seem to be friendly with one of the guards, and he brought her liquor in exchange for something. Elaine didn't want to think about what, though.

She sank to the floor again, dejected and too weak to move. She'd almost drifted off to sleep when more shouts sounded. They seemed to be coming closer.

"Get her out of here! Just take care of it, I don't want to deal with that woman anymore!"

Elaine sat up, slightly more alert. Who were they talking about?

"Janice!" she shouted.

"What?" roared a cranky, croaky voice.

"What's going on?"

"How should I know? Now shut up, my head is killing me!"

Elaine clutched the bars again and dragged herself to her feet, craning her neck to try to get a better view. A door slammed in the distance, and a man hurried from one hall to the other. She caught a slight glimpse of long, gray hair. Aggs!
Her heart pounded loudly in her ears, making her feel more ill than she already did.

"Help!" she shouted to no one in particular. Sobs overtook her as she realized the worst. Aggs had probably passed away. She rammed herself against the bars, desperate to see her one last time, but she couldn't do anything.

Suddenly, a man ran into the corridor from the back corner. He stopped directly in front of Elaine's cell. She flinched, expecting more beatings.

"Listen carefully, there's not much time," he whispered. "Vic and his cronies know something is up. We need to get you out of here."

"How can I trust you?" she shot back disgustedly.

"Because I knew your husband, Mitchell," he replied. "I'm one of *them*. And I'm on your side."

He took a small flashlight and flashed it over his eyes. They glittered eerily, and she could just catch a hint of red.

"But Aggs! What happened to Aggs?"

His face clouded over. "She…died. This morning. They're trying to bury her before a riot breaks out. Turns out she really had quite a few people who were on her side, and they're angry."

"I need to see her!"

"We can't. I've gotta get you out, reinforcements are on their way."

Before Elaine could protest, he unlocked the door and half-dragged, half-carried her out. He slipped her some water, making her feel instantly better. They hurried down the hall towards the main lobby while cries suddenly rose from the prisoners who were awake. Unable to wait for Elaine, the man scooped her up in his arms and ran through the dark halls.

Finally, they burst through some kind of back door and into the yard. A group of men were burying a woman with long gray hair. A sudden burst of energy overtook Elaine, angering her. She jumped from her rescuers' arms and flew at the men. Taken by surprise, the one digging dropped his shovel. Elaine picked it up and slammed it into his skull. As he dropped, she realized with horror that she might have killed him, but then she noticed his chest moving with breath. The other man headed towards her, only to be attacked from behind by the beast who'd released me. With an unearthly growl, he tackled the man and knocked him out with a massive blow to the head. Aggs dropped to the ground and rolled over, her long gray hair spilling over her pale face. Elaine hurried towards her, but a sudden sound by the gate froze her in her tracks.

"Mom?"

Elaine turned, hardly daring to believe her ears. A light-haired, almost blonde girl stood there, her piercing blue eyes staring at me.

"Lily?" I gasped. "Lily!"

She looked different, her hair was darker and her eyes were a strange, vivid blue, but it was definitely her. After these months of wondering, they'd finally found each other. Elaine ran to the gate, stumbling weakly, but she was able to reach through the bars and clasp Lily's hands in her own.

"Mom, you're so cold," Lily whispered, her face a mask of panic. "We've got to get you out of here!"

Before she could respond, the loud hum of a helicopter suddenly sounded above them. Elaine looked up in terror to see a small copter speeding through the air towards the prison.

"Stay right where you are!" commanded a loud voice over a speaker. Elaine knew that greasy voice. It had threatened and barked at her so many times she knew she'd never forget it.

"It's Vic!" Elaine shouted. "Run!"

Chapter Thirty-Seven
Lily

I barely had time to be happy about finding mom when the slime ball flew over in a helicopter. Mom shouted at me to run again, but I couldn't leave her again, not after all this searching. I was going to get her out of that stink hole if it killed me. Summoning all the anger I could, I stepped back and crouched down.

"Mom, back up!" I shouted over the noise of the blades.

"What are you doing?"

"Just back up!"

She ran towards the wall of the prison, stumbling often, her thin frame shaking from the early morning cold. She was terribly thin and pale, almost anorexic. What had they done to her?

My anger rose to a fever pitch as I ran towards the fence and slammed into it with all my might. Catching on, Barnwell and Jones did the same thing. Together, we smashed the fence until with an almighty groan, it crashed to the floor. Without hesitation, Jones jumped over the coil of charged wire and ran to my mother. He scooped her up in his arms and cradled her carefully as he ran pell-mell over the fence again, trying not to get blown over by the helicopter wind. Another man, holding Aggs, followed us. I was about to deck him when I realized by the glare of his eyes that he was a beast. He must have been the inside man.

"Mom!" I cried, trying not to lose myself and sob all over her. I hugged her close, alarmed by just how thin she felt in my arms.

She pulled back and looked me over critically. "You're skin and bones!" she sobbed. "What happened to you?"

"I'm fine, mom, what happened to you?" I hugged her again, suddenly frantic that I might lose her again. After all she'd been through, staying off the Mainframe's radar all these years, keeping a low profile, moving constantly, shielding me…and now, she'd clearly been starved and beaten. My anger started to rise again, and she noticed it in my eyes. Before she could say anything, however, a loud, arrogant voice sounded nearby.

"How very touching," Vic sneered as he walked across the yard towards us and stepped over the broken fence. I hadn't noticed the sudden quiet when the helicopter engine shut off. I clenched my hands into fists so hard that my jagged nails cut into my palms.

"If you know what's good for you, you'll get lost," I shouted.

"I wouldn't be giving me instruction if I were you, Mitchell," he hissed. "I've waited a long time for this moment. I knew if I set the bait, I'd catch you."

Suddenly, all rational thought flew from my mind. All I could think was how much I wanted to rip Vic's greasy throat out, pummel him, make him wish he'd never been born...

I sprang at him, ignoring the shouts behind me. I aimed for his stomach and missed his fist flying towards my cheek. He hit with sickening impact, making my cheek throb painfully as I fell towards the earth. I knew it would have hurt much worse without the Akrium in my system, but it still felt like someone had thrown a huge rock at my head.

"You think you know everything, don't you Mitchell?" He stepped over me, a manic, triumphant smile plastered across his disgusting face. "Well, now I've won, as I knew I would. Seems your boyfriend did a good job."

"What?" I asked dazedly.

"Your boyfriend. We enlisted him on a special mission, and he brought you back, just like we agreed. Although," he trailed off, looking at him, "he should be dead. It's been well over two weeks."

I lifted my head slightly and looked at Wes, who stared at Vic with pure hatred on his face. "Wes?" I asked timidly, terrified by what Vic said.

The anger in his face faltered for a moment as he looked at me. "Lily...they injected me with a tracker and told me to find you in two weeks or it would release poison and kill me."

"See?" Vic interrupted harshly. "Even your boyfriend was against you."

"They took it out in Epirus!" Wes shouted, the anger back. "You haven't won, Vic!"

Vic stepped over and punched Wes before he could defend himself. He stumbled quickly to his feet, but his nose bled profusely. He aimed a punch at Vic and managed a glancing blow, but Vic recovered quickly and landed a blow in his stomach. Wes crumpled to the floor, groaning.

So many things whirled through my thoughts that I could barely concentrate. Did Wes really betray me? Why hadn't he told me all this? But then why was he standing up to Vic for me?

I looked at Wes again, and my mom. They'd both been hurt, been put through so much because of me. I somehow found the strength to stand again, and lunged at Vic. I had the element of surprise on my side this time, and managed to nail him in the small of his back. He went sprawling face first in the dirt. I kicked him again in the ribs, my manic anger taking over again. A surge of heat shot from my core out through my limbs, giving me the most insane rush of power I'd ever felt. I turned him over and clutched his shirt, pulling him up from the ground while he spluttered in fear. With an inhuman roar, I threw him hard towards the barbed wire and felt a grim sort of satisfaction as he smashed into it with a sickening crunch.

I took a few deep breaths, overwhelmed all of a sudden with the adrenaline rush. Vic lay still, and for a fearful moment I wondered if I'd killed him. I hated him for everything he'd done to my family and I, but I couldn't cope with the thought that he might be dead at my hands.

"Lily?" came a timid voice behind me. I turned to see mom, tears streaming down her face, her frail frame shaking all over.

I stepped back, suddenly ashamed. "Mom...I...I'm sorry," I mumbled. "I don't know how to control it sometimes, I..."

A vicious growl suddenly sounded behind me. I turned to see Vic standing up, bleeding all over from cuts in the wire, but otherwise unharmed.

"You..."

"Thought you got me, did you?" he breathed, his hair now hanging in limp, greasy strings around his ears. "Two can play this game, Mitchell."

I swallowed hard, knowing immediately something was very, very wrong. "What do you mean?" I shot back, trying my hardest not to betray the fear welling inside me.

He reached into his pocket and grabbed a small vial. "I had a feeling I'd be meeting with you today," he sneered. "So I thought I'd take some time to prepare."

My heart pounding, I peered at the small black lettering on the vial. My heart caught in my throat as I figured out what it said.

"Akrium?" I replied shakily.

"Oh yes," he laughed. "Now I'm just as strong as you are."

Chapter Thirty-Eight
Lily

I stared in disbelief, unable to believe my eyes. Gleefully, Vic took a small, silver object from his pocket and raised it to his lips. He blew a loud note on it and folded his arms, a look of smug satisfaction on his face. Men in full black uniform and gear suddenly jumped from the roof of the prison or jumped out of other hiding places. Some rose up from the streets like a horrible black wave of death. They swarmed us and put us in cuffs.

"Take all of them to the Mainframe. I have a little plan I think they'll fit nicely into." Vic roared with laughter as he followed the black-clad entourage to the Mainframe building. My heart sank lower with each step, knowing I'd failed everyone, knowing that we'd come so close to freedom only to fall short at the finish line.

As we walked, I noticed that my captor stayed oddly close to me. We came to the courtyard of the Mainframe, and he suddenly pulled me back.

"Listen carefully if you want to live," he whispered in my ear. "Vic will take you, run some tests and then kill you. He needs you to build a super army. Epirus's ground forces are far better than ours, and that's why we're losing the war."

"So?" I hissed back, in no mood for codes or secret plans or anything anymore.

"So you won't have a chance to rescue your family. I'm on your side. I'm going to release you. As soon as I do, run behind the memorial wall on the north side of the building for cover. You'll need it."

"What about the others? I'm not leaving without them."

"They've been warned too. You must do as I say. Don't waste any time. Do you understand?"

My heart began to race. "Yeah," I replied tersely. I heard a small click, and the shackles dropped from my wrists.

"GO!" he whispered loudly, prodding me in the back. I took off and ran for the appointed place as shouts rose up behind me. I turned back for a brief second to see Wes, mom, Barnwell and Jones running the same direction, urging me on. I pushed myself harder, running for all I was worth to the wall.

A loud blast suddenly sounded as we all huddled behind the memorial, making me go temporarily deaf. The force of the shockwave pushed me off my feet, taking my breath away. I found Wes and clung to him for all I was worth. He wrapped his arms around me protectively, then reached out for my mom nearby and protected her too.

The ringing in my ears finally subsided, and I untangled myself from Wes. I bit back a scream as I peeked around the corner. The Mainframe, barely held together by the joints and beams, had been bombed from the inside. Fire poured from some of the upper windows. I looked to the courtyard and saw several of the black clad men, seemingly fighting with each other.

I looked back at Wes, who wore a wide grin.

"What's going on?" I shouted, still a little deaf.

"The resistance! It's starting!" he cried.

"The what?"

"The Underground Movement, remember? They must have been engineering this for weeks!" He let out a gleeful laugh, sounding so relieved and happy that I couldn't help but feel the same way.

I looked back and noticed with a shock that Avery and Trent were pushing their way through the fray, accompanied by several beasts. The beasts flicked aside the men fighting them like flies. I noticed some were still bald, but the awful red glare was gone from their eyes. They fought magnificently, seeming never to tire.

Trent and Avery reached us at the wall and gave everyone hugs. As Avery embraced my mom, she turned to me.

"Is this your mother?" Avery asked. I nodded, still a little too overwhelmed to speak. She smiled, then hugged me.

"Thank you," she whispered. I pulled away and looked at her.

"For what?"

"For saving me. And Trent."

She gave my hand a quick squeeze, then looked at Barnwell and Jones. "You know the plan?" she asked them. They nodded somberly and stood up, pulling small, square objects from their hands.

"Long distance Tasers," Avery explained. "They can paralyze someone up to twenty feet away."

"Oh. Um…ok," I replied, not really knowing what to say and feeling confused as ever.

"Be safe, Lily," she said, then turned and headed back into the hysteria with Trent. I looked to Barnwell and Jones.

"They've rigged the trains, so we've got a ride heading north to headquarters right now," said Jones. "Everything is ours now. It's taken years of planning, but we've finally done it."

He grinned broadly and nudged Barnwell. "Let's get going."

"Wait…what? What's going on?" I asked.

"We'll explain it on the way," said Barnwell. "But we've got to move."

* * *

Half an hour later, our train, filled to capacity with scared refugees, pulled out of the station and headed north. Barnwell and Jones instructed us to get as many innocent people as we could on board and get them across the border.

"Border? What border?" asked Wes.

"The northern border," said Jones. "The north side officially seceded a couple days ago after building a border. They didn't want anything to do with Vic or the south anymore. They threatened to overthrow, and Vic planned to invade until a certain girl came into the picture."

He winked at me, and it suddenly hit me. I'd been an integral part of the plan all along. My coming to the city opened the way for the rebellion to start. I started to feel a little dizzy and sat back down in my chair by the window.

"So…what do we do now?" asked mom.

"We're going to Underground Headquarters. You'll learn more there."

It wasn't the full explanation I'd been hoping for, but at least we were on our way. A few men suddenly stepped into our car, carrying a body wrapped loosely in some clean sheets. They laid her down on a long table in the room.

"This is Agatha," said one of the men. "Word on the street is that she knew you two well."

He looked directly at me. I stifled tears as I looked down at the small body, but mom let loose. The two must have gotten to know each other well while she was in prison.

"Would you like to say a few words, ma'am?" said the man who'd carried Aggs. "Aggs was one of our biggest advocates, even back when the Underground Movement started."

Mom stepped forward, drying her eyes and trying to regain control. "I don't know exactly what to say. Aggs saved my life. She watched over my daughter. She…was the best person I've ever known."

She dissolved into sobs again. I walked close to her and put my arms around her shoulders. Each person in the room bowed their heads in silent prayer.

"Let's bury her up north," I said after a while. "She was born there, and I think that's what she would have wanted."

Everyone mumbled assent, then gradually dissipated. The men who'd carried Aggs took her to another car to be dressed for burial. I stayed close to mom until she fell asleep on one of the reclining seats, then moved closer to Wes, who stood by a window.

"You ok?" I asked.

He looked at me, then wrapped his arms around my waist and pulled me close. "Well…I'm not going to lie. I was a little freaked out by what you did to Vic."

I looked up at him. "Well, I'm a little freaked out by what you were going to do to me."

"Lily, about that…I promise I had no intention of bringing you back to him. They put me in that position, just like he said, but I'd already determined I'd die before I hurt you."

I held him closer and stroked his cheek with my fingers. "I know…it's just been hard to know who to trust anymore. I know I went psycho and scared you. I just can't control myself sometimes. The Akrium takes over everything when I get really angry."

"I guess it isn't like he didn't deserve it," he replied with a shadow of his old smile. He bent down and kissed me softly.

I stared out the window again, glad to be safe and have my family and loved ones with me, but I still felt a little empty inside for some reason. The landscape that passed was burned, dead and depressing. So much uncertainty still lay ahead.

But then I looked at Wes and felt fully how much I really loved him. As I held his warm hand in mine, I tried to hold onto the hope that at least this time, I wouldn't face the unknown alone.

Epilogue
Vic

The cursed girl once again got away. Vic sat up angrily from where he laid on the concrete, watching his empire, his glory, burn away.

Those who were wounded lay uselessly along the sidewalk, while those who'd survived the encounter went after the others, the freaks. He thought he'd finally gotten rid of them, sending them into exile where they were sure to face certain death. The makeshift border made by the northern country bumpkins had beaten them back, and the so-called Underground movement had finally laid out their plans and executed them.

Vic stood up, cringing a little as he put weight on his sprained ankle, but he knew it would soon heal. The Akrium coursing through him would do that.

And those beasts! How did they look so healthy? The Akrium should have killed them long ago. Though Vic could feel the power of it coursing through his veins, he also felt the destruction it did to his body. His eyes had turned a horrible blood red, glittering every time he got angry or felt any emotion at all. His hair had begun to fall out in large clumps, his skin yellowing into a strange, unearthly, pasty color. Yet those beasts seemed…normal. They'd gotten with *the girl* somehow, figured out the secret, and Vic was determined to have it. But how?

He limped his way back to the Mainframe, trying to sort out a plan, when he felt a tap on his arm. He whirled angrily, expecting to see some timid little urchin from the ranks, needing instructions for every step they took, every blink of their pathetic eyes, but he only saw a bald man with eyes that glittered eerily.

"Vic Channing?" he asked with a horrible leer. For a moment, Vic felt a small twinge of fear, but brushed it aside as he remembered who he was and the power he now possessed. He'd poisoned President Rhone slowly, so slowly and imperceptibly nobody had noticed. He'd taken charge when no one else would. He was Vic Channing, and nothing could stop him now.

"Yes. You are?" he asked curtly, making his impatience obvious.

"Name's Lycus," the man replied.

He didn't say anything more, so Vic shrugged, irritated. "And?"

"And I believe I can help you," he replied. From his pocket, he pulled a small vial of clear liquid. "Do you know what this is?"

"No," Vic replied, rolling his eyes.

"This," the beast said with a vicious grin, "is the cure."

Brittiany West is the author of several short stories, a novella and
two novels. She began her writing career as a reporter and
columnist for a small town newspaper. The Shadowlands Series
are her breakout novels. Mrs. West lives in Ohio with her husband
and five children.

Printed in Great Britain
by Amazon.co.uk, Ltd.,
Marston Gate.